Leather Spirit Stallion

Leather Spirit Stallion

by Raven Kaldera

Circlet Press, Inc.
Cambridge, MA

Leather Spirit Stallion
by Raven Kaldera

Copyright © 2014 Circlet Press, Inc.
Cover art © 2014 Brandon Hardy

First paperback edition, December 2014
ISBN 978-1-61390-131-1

Published by Circlet Press, Inc.
39 Hurlbut Street
Cambridge, MA 02138

Author's Note: This is a work of fiction. While it has been created with the help and advice of representatives of the various Asian-American cultures represented here, it is still, in essence, a work of fiction. Any resemblance to people real or imagined is purely coincidental. Don't go around expecting individuals in the various cultures represented to resemble the characters in this story.

Leather Spirit Stallion

Chapter One

The boots, as he pulled them on, were new to his feet, although not new themselves. They were military tanker's boots, black leather with buckles. He had scammed them off of Chaz, who had money and was continually buying fancy pieces of black leather and then getting bored with them. The pants, too, were black leather, found in the local Salvation Army a year ago. The belt had been his older brother's until he had stolen it, just before leaving his parents' house forever.

Aside from that, the rest of his clothing didn't resemble anything that someone might wear to a fetish bar. Over a simple sleeveless black T-shirt he shrugged on and tied his black silk *del*, the traditional Mongolian coat with fur trim. He had stitched it himself, scavenging the fur from an abandoned coat in the trash, learning to embroider the traditional patterns onto it. Unlike his ceremonial *del*, which was a feast of bright colors, the black *del* was more demure with embroidery only in indigo and white. The running horse tracked across his sleeves, his spirit animal in silver-gray. The broad silk sash of cobalt blue went around his waist and tied, then he buckled the leather belt around it. He picked up his sheath knife and hesitated for a moment, then tucked it into his boot. Wearing it at the waist was more traditional, but discreet was better; he didn't want it confiscated by a bouncer. He picked up his handmade horsehair whip and fastened that to his belt instead. *Read that message, boys.*

There was no mirror and it was getting dark in his tent, but he quickly brushed out his straight jet-black hair, which now reached well past his shoulders. His mother had never allowed long hair in her house; as soon as he had walked out of there, he had sworn that the next time scissors touched his hair would be a trim when it reached his waist. Brushing the front part back severely from his face, he tied it into a long-stemmed horsetail on the top of his head with a red leather thong wrapped around several times, then added an ornament of dangling bones. Let them wonder. He knew what they would see in this new leather bar—a not-very-tall young Asian-American man with long hair, and not in any kind of a stereotypical leather costume, at least not from the waist up. They would probably decide that he was a submissive, based solely on his height, build, and race; far too many drunken queens assumed that any Asian man in a bar under the age of forty was a desperate Southeast Asian hustler out to suck cock for a few dollars. He would probably have to fight to prove otherwise. He'd had to do that, in the gay leather bar that closed down in his parents' town. Of course, then he'd been underage and using a fake ID, stealing out at night on a quest for the sexual fantasies that spun through his head. He hadn't found them, but he'd learned a lot.

Taking a deep breath, he looked around the darkness of his tent one more time. Reaching in the dark for his lighter and the bowl with the stick of dried juniper, he lit the stick for a moment and swung it around himself three times, softly chanting "*Hurai, hurai, hurai.* Golden-edged Golomto, daughter of heaven, I ask your blessing. *Hurai, hurai, hurai.*" He waved the stick nine times in the direction of his altar and then blew it out. Then he put the sacred incense reverently down in front of the altar, invisible in the darkness, and stepped out of his tent.

The glow of the streetlights greeted him from beyond the three-story apartment building. His *ger*—the traditional Mongolian tent—was kept in a storage area in back of the building, surrounded by a chainlink fence. He couldn't afford even the small apartment that he'd rented on the third floor; it was more cost-effective to sublet it to his friends Mike and Jerry, with a deal to be allowed to use the bathroom whenever he wanted to, and pitch his homemade *ger* in the back storage area that he'd talked the landlord into adding to the lease for an extra twenty dollars. *I keep camping equipment in there. Yeah, and a barbecue. I like to have that little square of asphalt to smoke my steaks.* No one had to know that he was living there. The padlock clicked in place with a prayer to the spirits to keep his living space safe, and then he got onto his bicycle and flew.

In his mind, he thought of the bike as his horse, although the experience was entirely different from actual horseback riding. He supposed that a motorcycle would be more horselike in some ways, but at the moment he couldn't afford one of those either. Being a college student on financial aid, living on a tiny stipend each month so that he wouldn't have to ask a cent of his parents, one had to put up with a certain amount of austerities. His food was taken care of on campus, and he could have lived there for free except that he couldn't imagine how it would work. Living with his altar and all his spirits, doing chanting ritual almost daily, going into trance where interruptions could be dangerous—this did not square well with being crowded into a tiny dorm room with an incredulous roommate. At least the *ger* was roomy and private, even if it was going to be chilly when winter came. *Some of your ancestors were probably reindeer people from Siberia, you idiot. You think they'll be sympathetic to you whining that your tent is cold?*

The city lights whizzed by as he ducked in and out of traffic. Bicycling to and from school—and everywhere else—had given his body more whiplike muscles, but he knew he'd never be particularly large. *It doesn't matter. Dominance is in the eye and the mind, not the frame. And I am a descendant of Chingghis Khan.* At least he figured that it was a good bet, being that the Human Genome Project had clocked eight percent of Asia as being descended from Genghis, as Europeans called him, and his various sons. Anyway, he'd dreamed of being a *buu*, a Mongol shaman, since he was fourteen, so he figured that it was probably the old blood surfacing somewhere.

The new *Black Hawk* boasted a line of shiny motorcycles chained to the railing outside, like quiescent metal chargers waiting for their black knights. He pulled up and got off his secondhand bike, sighing, and stared at them enviously. *You are a buu,* he reminded himself. *You have more windhorse than any of those fuckers. Don't chicken out* now. *Meet them on your own terms, or not at all.* Gritting his teeth, he padlocked his bicycle next to the motorbikes—he thought of it briefly as a little Mongolian pony next to the big European chargers, and the thought ran through his head: *We conquered half the world on those little ponies, and your big old ancestors ran before us like sheep.* Lifting his head high, he walked quickly for the door, the skirts of his *del* swirling around his calves.

There was a line, with five or six moustached men in leather waiting to get past the ticket-taker. They looked at him curiously as he came up behind them, but he avoided their gazes and kept his face rigid. *Inscrutable Asian, right?* The ticket man passed them in and he flipped his ID into the drawer along with the bar entry fee.

The man behind the glass blinked at him, then stared at his ID, then stared back at him. "Er-lik So-long-o," he sounded out. "This your real name?"

It is now. Sure, it used to be Eric James Chang, but the name change was legal before I transferred colleges. "Yes," he said, unblinking.

The ticket man stared at him some more, making him wonder briefly if the guy was drunk on duty. "What kind of a name is that?" he finally asked.

"Buryat." He knew that wouldn't make sense to the man, but felt perverse enough to say it anyway. Then he added, "Mongolian."

"Oh. Like Genghis Khan, right?"

He bared his teeth in something that wasn't a smile. "Yes. Like Chinggis."

"Oh, right. I like your costume."

"It isn't a costume." He held out his hand. "Are you going to give me a ticket, or what?"

The man seemed to suddenly remember what his job was. "Oh, right. Here." He pushed Erlik's ID back through the glass with a ticket. Erlik gave a formal nod of his head—he'd learned that even a small bow was seen as subservient in these places—and strode on into the bar.

It was a fundraiser night—thus the door fee—and the place

was crawling with leather clones. He looked for a barstool, but they were all taken, so he found a piece of wall and leaned against it, arms crossed. For now, he would survey the territory, and see if there was anything worth hunting.

"Nice costume," said a voice next to him, over the loud music. He turned his head sharply, in a single jerked movement like an owl—he'd learned that this, combined with a deadpan stare, kept people off balance. The leather-clad man next to him stepped back just a little as he turned his gaze on him. *Good. Distance is respect.*

"Not a costume," Erlik said. "This is what I wear every day. Or something like it." He jerked up the hem of his *del* to reveal the leather pants and boots beneath it. "That part is the costume."

"Wow," the guy said, completely missing the reference to his own leather pants. "So where are you from?"

Meaning, what country, and how did you get such a good American accent? "Fresno," he said, with just a hint of sarcasm.

There was a guffaw from his other side, which stopped as his head jerked around in that direction. A tall broad man was drinking from a stein of beer and grinning at him. "They dress like that in Fresno?" he asked.

"No. Not unless there are others there like me and I don't know about them. Which I doubt." He kept his voice even, his face impassive.

"People like you?" the first guy asked, curious.

Erlik gave a small shrug. "I'm a *buu*. That's the Mongolian word for a shaman. Like a medicine man, only from Asia," he added in case these guys were the sort who didn't even know that anyone other than Native Americans had spirit-workers.

"...And you're in a gay bar?" the man with the beer asked, his eyes crinkling at the corners.

He shrugged again. "There's no law saying that shamans have to be straight. In fact, that's where a lot of queerfolk ended up in the old days."

"What's that?" The first man flinched when Erlik's head

snapped back toward him. He had been pointing at the horsehair whip. With one hand, Erlik unfastened it from his belt and whipped it downward across his leather boot. It made a satisfying crack against the leather, and several people looked around to find the source of the sound.

"Horsehair," he said, clipping it back to his belt. "Made from the tails of seven stallions." That much was absolutely true. The one good thing that his parents had done for him was to pay for all those horseback riding lessons in his teens, so that he could walk into the campus stables with experience and get a part-time job shoveling manure and occasionally teaching a beginner to ride. It was easy to gather shed tail hairs from the few uncastrated male horses and braid them into a multi-tailed whip in his spare time.

"Wow," said the first guy again. "Can I see it?"

Erlik looked at him levelly. "No."

"So you're a top," the beer guy said.

He let a slow smile creep across his face, the first expression it had worn since he'd walked in. "In Mongolian, the word *dom* means a magic spell," he said, one hand still on his whip.

Both were silent for a moment, and then the beer guy held out a hand. "Curt," he said. "Switch. Usually."

"Erlik." He shook the burly man's hand.

"Air-leek?" asked the denim guy, looking bemused. He didn't introduce himself, just bounced on his toes a little and asked, "Will you top me? I was supposed to meet this guy Rand, but he's not coming and I'd hate to have to go home without any action."

Erlik looked at him, calculating the trouble of beating someone so clueless against the disappointment of turning down what might possibly be the only offer he'd be given—and then recalculating that equation with the added variable of looking too desperate. After several seconds of silence, the denim guy was starting to look antsy, but then Curt drew his attention by clearing his throat. "Actually, I was hoping that I could—um—talk to you about some of your, you know, Mongolian stuff." The subtle emphasis was clearly a message, and while Erlik wasn't entirely sure what the message was, he was willing to trust it.

"Maybe later," he said, cracking his mask and favoring the denim guy with a one-sided smile.

The nameless guy shrugged. "Okay. See ya round." He wandered off, and Erlik turned back to Curt, who shrugged, with a bit of a sheepish smile.

"Jeffy's a doofus," Curt said. "Not a bad guy, but he's not serious about anything, you know? And you look like a serious guy. I figured I'd spare you."

Erlik gave him a nod of thanks. "Was that all, or did you actually have something you wanted to ask me?"

Curt hesitated, and Erlik braced himself for the rejection, but then the bigger man said, "You said that you were like a medicine man, right? Or some kind of psychic?"

"Something like that. You could call me a shaman, but the actual word is *buu*."

The bigger man hesitated again, and then said, "I'm really worried about my ex. He's dropped out of sight and I'm worried that he's using again. I don't know whether to go looking for him or leave it alone. Whether he's in trouble or not."

Erlik's breath whooshed out of him. *Work. Work has come to find me, when I just wanted a night out. Spirits, sometimes you are bitches.* He closed his eyes, and then opened them again, focusing on the fluorescent lights. "I can try to help you, yes. But not here, in the bar. You'd need to come to me for that."

Curt tilted up the last swig of his beer. "Can we go to your place now? This place is a graveyard tonight, and the more I think about Jason, the less I want to be here. I'll pay your entry fee," he said.

"You'd need to pay me more than that," Erlik said. "I am a professional. I do charge for these things. It's negotiable—even barter would do—but you'd have to pay me what you thought it was worth."

Curt looked at him, looked down, flushed, and then asked, "Would you be interested in taking it out in trade? I'm told I'm a decent bottom."

Perhaps the spirits aren't such bitches after all. "We can do that," he said. "That would work out very well, in fact."

It took an hour to get the right combination of buses back to Erlik's place—Curt had come on public transport, which meant Erlik had to stow his bike on the bus and ride back with him. The bigger man did look rather uneasy when Erlik led him around to the chainlink fence and clicked open the padlock. *Perhaps he thinks that I'm an Asian gang member, and ninjas are going to come pouring out and abduct him.* "Wait here for a minute," he said. "I'm going to go in and get a fire lit, get us some light." Just to make sure that the man didn't chicken out and run away, he relocked the padlock behind them, and then ducked into the black *ger*. A match lit the fire in his hibachi, and then he lit the lantern hanging from the ceiling and the candles on his altar. "Come on in," he said, opening the doorflap.

Curt came in warily, glancing around as if for the nonexistent ninjas, and then his eyes widened when he took in the tent. Under the plastic tarp and the coarse black fabric of the homemade *ger*, the circular tent was decorated with painted hangings of spirits and symbols. A wooden cot with a narrow futon took up one corner, and the altar took up the other side. A cooler and a few boxes, and another embroidered *del* hanging over the bed, were the only other items to be seen. The asphalt under their feet had been spray-painted with a circular pattern of stick-figure horses and men, copied from the top of an ancient spirit drum. "Wow," he said, staring at the altar with its figurines and candles and bowls and ribbons. "This is... quite a setup. You're really a...."

"Yes." Erlik pulled three sheepskins off of the pile at the foot of his cot and laid them end-to-end on the ground. Then he picked up the bag with his *shagai*, his four yak anklebones, and sat down cross-legged on one sheepskin. "Take off your shoes and sit down," he said. "Ask your question."

Curt awkwardly got his boots off—Erlik smiled to see that he didn't argue about the fact that Erlik had remained booted—and sat on the third sheepskin, across from him. He took a deep breath. "I want to know if Jason is all right," he said. "If he's in trouble. How he's doing."

The bones rattled in Erlik's hand and fell. "One camel and three goats," he said. "Not good news. Usually illness or failure." He held his hand over the bones and closed his eyes. *Tell me, spirits. How does his friend do?*

It was Uncle Gavia who answered, Uncle who'd been the first spirit to speak to him, late at night while he lay awake in his parents' house. Uncle who'd said, *I claim you. You are my descendant through many generations, and you will take up the drum that my other descendants have laid down.* At first he thought that he was crazy, hearing things, but eventually Uncle proved himself to be quite real. As did the ones who followed him.

He is ill, said Uncle. *Not doing the drugs, but drinking instead. And not caring for his body. He wants to die.* Erlik heard the words coming out of his mouth.

Curt looked unhappy. "Should I go to him?" The bones clicked and fell again.

"Two horses, two camels," he said. "All things successful. Go to him. He misses you. Save his life." He looked at Curt. "Tomorrow. He will not die tonight, and now you owe me."

Curt swallowed, his attitude entirely different from when they were standing in the bar. Now they were on Erlik's turf, in a shaman's *ger*, and the burly man seemed smaller somehow. "What now?" he asked.

"Now you take off your clothes," Erlik said, gesturing to his cot, "fold them, and put them there. And then I give you a beating." He stood and stepped back. Curt got up slowly, eyeing him, then began to take his jacket off.

"You're not going to go psycho on me, are you?" he asked

dubiously.

That cracked Erlik's dispassionate mask and brought a burst of laughter from him. "You think I'd say yes if I was?" he asked.

Curt grinned sheepishly. "Yeah, I guess not. That was kind of stupid." He began to strip off his clothing; his bare skin gleamed in the firelight as more of it was exposed. Erlik's breath came harder, and he grabbed and untwisted one of the lengths of black rope that he kept under the bed. *Maybe this is actually going to work out.* He stepped up onto the cot, where he was taller than the other man and could reach the tent beams.

Curt held out his forearms, and Erlik bound them together with the black rope, then threw the end over the beams at the top of the *ger*. He knew they could bear the man's weight, because he'd done this before. Once, anyway. Tying it off to a lower beam, he asked, "Is that too tight?"

"No, that's fine," said Curt.

Erlik looked down at him from the height of the cot. "No, what?" he asked.

Curt ducked his head. "No, sir," he said in a low voice.

"Better." He jumped down off the cot and circled around behind the taller man. He was stocky and had a beer belly, but his ass was well shaped. "Can you refrain from screaming loud enough to wake my neighbors, or are you going to require a gag of some sort?" he asked courteously.

Curt blinked, and then said, "Depends on how hard you're going to hit me. Sir," he added.

Erlik smiled at him. "Better get a gag, then." He reached over and grabbed Curt's underwear off the bed and stuffed it into his mouth, then grabbed up a leather thong and tied it in place. "I find it's always useful to have something to bite down on." Then he picked up the horsehair whip and made it whisk through the air, letting the tails just touch Curt as they went by. As he hoped, the man flinched even though it wasn't hard enough to hurt. *Anticipation is good.* Then he drew back and hit him in earnest.

The bigger man stayed stoic through the first several blows, but eventually he began to make noise, his body arching with the pain.

Erlik circled him, decorating his chest and the front of his thighs, but not hitting his genitals. Yet. He circled back to his ass and shoulders, the backs of his thighs. Curt began to make serious noise at that point, moving away from the whip. Reaching around to his front, his tormentor grabbed the base of his cock and balls, holding him in one place while he laid into his ass all the harder. The man jumped and whimpered and made hooting noises behind the gag, writhing in Erlik's grip. Eventually, when his ass was flaming red, it was abandoned and Erlik moved again to face him.

"Now the even more fun part," he said, and tied the leather thong around the base of Curt's cock and balls, winding it around them. The man hung in the rope bondage, waiting, watching his erect cock jutting from the coils of leather. Erlik slid the tails of the horsehair whip through his hands—one of the things he loved about it was that it could strike hard or lightly with a great range of sensations—and then, without warning, flicked it at Curt's genitals.

The man flinched and let out a cry, but as Erlik looked up at him, making eye contact, he moved his pelvis back to where it had been, offering them again. *Good.* Erlik brushed the ends of the tails along it, bringing out a whimper, and then struck again, this time on his balls. Lighter than he'd hit the cock, but it wouldn't feel that way. Again the flinch and cry, again the man found his balance and brought himself back to the center to take another blow. Erlik sped up the blows, slowly, until Curt was bracing himself with bent legs and his head thrown back, tears running down his face as his genitals took the punishment.

Then Erlik decided that he'd had enough, because his own cock was so hard that it was distracting, and protruding beneath the waistband of his pants. Tossing aside the whip, he undid and stripped off his *del*, and then his T-shirt. He untied Curt's hands from the beam above and helped to lower the trembling man to the sheepskins on the floor, "Steady, steady," he whispered. "There, just stay like that." On his knees, bent forward.

Erlik retied the rope to one of the vertical posts so that his hands were stretched out in front of him and he was on his elbows, and then rubbed the man's flaming ass with his hand.

Curt made a mewling noise, but pushed his ass into Erlik's touch; one hand grabbed for the lube under the edge of the bed, and worked a palmful into Curt's ass. It opened up easily—he was obviously no virgin, which was fine with Erlik. Teasing a virgin open was something he'd done once, and while it was thrilling in its own way, a quick fuck was a lot better with someone who knew how to relax and open up. He got his pants open and his cock out, got the last condom out of his pocket and onto his cock with only a little bit of fumbling—which Curt couldn't see, thank the Gods that tops could hide that sort of thing—and then slowly slid himself into Curt's ass.

The man let out a low moan, the first of that sort of sound he'd made all night. Rather than letting loose with an immediate pounding, Erlik restrained himself and worked his cock more slowly in and out of the man's ass until he was squirming and making *more-more-more* noises. Then it was a hard, bouncing ride, and at one point Erlik reached under Curt's beer belly and grabbed his cock, which came practically immediately in his hand. He wiped the come on Curt's writhing, groaning ass and grabbed his hips, pumping himself quickly into the other man until he came himself.

Then there was the untying, and letting Curt move and groan and get a swig of water from Erlik's jug, and checking out all his reddened areas to make sure that none of them were bleeding, and disposing of the condoms—"Can I have yours? As a souvenir, I keep them," asked Curt, but Erlik turned him down; his seed could too easily be used against him and he didn't want it to fall into the wrong hands. Curt wriggled on the sheepskins and stared up at the tent roof, saying, "Wow, man, that was cool, but this place is sure weird." He laughed. "Shaman sex!"

"That wasn't shaman sex," said Erlik. "That was just a beating and a fuck, for fun. If we'd had shaman sex, you'd be bound to me forever." He grinned at the expression on the other man's face. "Don't worry. You're free to go. And I thank you for giving me this small part of you."

Curt held his eyes and nodded, slowly. "You know, I think

that I believe you," he said. He averted his eyes, uncomfortably, toward the altar where the candles were still shimmering. "All the time that you were beating me, I was feeling like someone was watching me from over there."

"They were," said Erlik. "But don't worry about it. They mean you no harm, and some of the energy went to them, anyway."

"Uh," said Curt. "Okay. Anyway, that's what I felt. And it made me, you know, not want to cop out when it hurt a lot."

"The spirits have that effect on people," said Erlik casually. *And tomorrow you'll decide that it was all crazy, and you'll convince yourself that you were imagining things. And that won't matter, because I got what I came for.* He nodded and stood up. "Shall I find a pay phone and call you a cab?" he asked.

"Nah, I'm fine. I'll walk to the bus stop, it'll do me good to stretch my legs. And I should be getting home." He looked around one more time, with a glance that Erlik translated as, *I'm glad that I don't have to spend the night in this creepy place,* and got up to find his clothing.

Later, in the night, Alma Mergen came to Erlik while he was dreaming. She was a powerful spirit, and one who rarely came unless something was important. Her long black hair swept the asphalt ground of his tent, and her sky-blue robes trailed behind her. She held a knife and a drum, warrioress and shamaness. *You are a hunter,* she said, *but you hunt only small prey. You must hunt something greater to earn what you need. The time will come, soon, to be brave, horse-child.* But in the morning he remembered her visit, but not her words.

Chapter Two

The next morning he left earlier than necessary to get over to the science building—he had a part-time job cleaning up the labs, and needed to put in an hour on it before the morning class began. He needed the money badly; he was running short of incense and cash for the laundry machines. As he pulled up to the campus on his bike, a conflagration of police and sirens and crowds of students welcomed him. The science building was cordoned off, and people milled about, watching. He saw a classmate in the crowd and hurried over. "What the—"

"Guy with a gun. Some grad student gone nuts. Holding a bunch of freshmen hostage." The girl never took her eyes off of the windows.

"Great. So much for cleaning out the labs." Erlik shook his head, refiguring his pocket change in his mind to see if it would stretch out for the week. "No matter what happens no one's getting any classes there for a week. Hey, do the cops know about the way in behind the bushes—" He broke off, realizing that there was no point in talking out loud around people who weren't listening anyway. *Maybe I should just go up to the ropes and ask the police if they know about the way through the iron gate.* The gate was overgrown with thorny bushes on either side; the ground staff never seemed to get around to dealing with them. Dumpsters also blocked the way these days, but he'd gotten quietly in and out a few times during his homeless period. The gate opened onto the courtyard in the middle of the science building, and you could see all the inner rooms from there.

Making his way to the police barrier, he followed the yellow plastic cordon until he got around to the back. There was a cop there, but Erlik couldn't get his attention—too busy talking into the mic in his ear. Then he heard the voice, clear as day, right over his left shoulder. *You should go in there.*

"I can't," he whispered aloud. "There are cops. There's a gunman."

You should go in there. He's in there. You can help.

Erlik shook his head. "How can I help? I'm an apprentice *buu,* not a warrior." *Not a warrior,* he thought again, bitterly. *No matter how tough I may act in a leather bar. I'm not a martial artist or anything. And what do you mean by 'he?' A nutball with a gun?* "Thanks, I'll just stay right here," he whispered, his words lost in the noise of the crowd.

Go in. We watch your back. Go in.

"No," he said, louder, but then the cop suddenly moved further away and the dumpster area was left unguarded. An ambulance blew by, heading for the front of the building with sirens howling, and everyone looked in that direction. "This is crazy," he said, but found himself ducking under the yellow tape and walking briskly toward the dumpster area. No one noticed him, including the policeman, which was a miracle. His heart was pounding in his chest by the time he ducked behind the dumpster, just a dozen steps away. *A guy dressed in weird Asian clothing strolls right by a cop and a crowd of onlookers and they don't notice. Damn, Uncle, you do good work.*

There was a large piece of heavy plastic behind the dumpster that had been there since the last time he'd tried to crawl through these bushes, months ago. Wrapping himself thoroughly in two layers of it—he'd breathe when he got through to the other side— he pushed his way through the thorns and put his body weight against the gate. It wasn't surprising that the police hadn't noticed this door yet, although it was likely that the janitors would have told them soon enough. *Just as well that I'm doing this quickly instead of waiting,* he thought, and then shook his head under the plastic. *This is nuts. Evading cops, evading crazed gunmen, what am I thinking? What if they think I'm the gunman, or his accomplice?* He got through the gate and shed the plastic, forcing himself to take deep breaths. *Don't think about that. Uncle and the others are behind me. Where do I go now?*

He crouched down and scanned the rows of windows, still

half-crouched behind the second layer of bushes. No way to tell which was the room with gunmen and hostages. Doubt assailed him; perhaps he should have wandered about and asked, perhaps someone would have known.... No. There was a sense of urgency about this. *People are going to die,* said Uncle. *Use the tools you have.*

Scanning the classroom windows again, he noticed that they were all tilted open to get air in the warm morning, except for one set on the second floor that was shut tight. As he looked at them, a chill ran through his belly. *That's where he is,* said Uncle. *That's where you need to go.*

He chewed his lip, thinking. There was no point trying to go through the halls and come in the door; that would just get him shot. Coming in the wide classroom windows would be equally deadly, and anyhow they were shut now. But behind each of the large science classrooms was the lab closet, a small room lined with shelves and storage. *That would be the little window right there. Bet he hasn't even thought about that. Right.*

Taking off his boots, he tied them together and slipped the knot through his belt. His socks followed, tucked into his boots, and in bare feet he climbed the stonework to the ledge under the window, bare toes clutching at the rough concrete. The second-floor window of the lab closet was unlocked, as he knew it would be. It wasn't hard to open it quietly, little by little, and silently wriggle through. *There are some benefits to being a smaller guy,* he thought wryly. He could hear voices on the other side, or one voice, anyway, although he couldn't hear what it was saying.

He knew what he'd find in this lab closet, because it was one of the ones he cleaned. Next to the window was a thick twin-size mattress, standing on its end; students had used it to bounce weights off of in some experiment. There was also a toolbox, and he could reach it from where he stood on the inside windowsill. He opened it, carefully, and took out two hammers; tucking them in his belt, he climbed up on the top edge of the mattress. It almost buckled under his weight—almost, not quite, if he kept his feet spread wide apart and held onto the wall as best he could.

He could hear the voice in the next room fairly clearly now, and it seemed to be a one-sided conversation, probably with some hostage negotiator on the other end of a phone. "I told you not to go into the building! Any of you!" the voice shrieked, almost sobbing. "I told you that if one of you went through that door, someone was going to get shot! You'd better fucking get all your people out of here, right now, or someone dies! I mean it! Don't fuck with me, I saw them go in! Don't fuck with me!" And then there was a gunshot, echoing through the room, and a rough high-pitched cry, followed by the screams of girls. Erlik's stomach contracted, and he almost fell off of his precarious perch on the mattress. *Oh gods. What am I doing here?*

Now, said Uncle, urgently in his ear. *Now, when he's just shot someone and he's not thinking clearly. Get his attention. Now!* The voice harried him, but he couldn't seem to move. Then one of the hammers slipped out of his belt and fell to the floor of the lab closet with a clatter.

His breath stopped and the blood roared in his ears. There was a mumble outside, and then the doorknob rattled, the door banged open. A nondescript-looking young man with thick glasses came in, a handgun pointed in one hand and a rifle slung over his shoulder. *Don't look up, don't look up,* Erlik prayed. *There is nothing up here, all the interesting things are down low—and over there, where all the shelves are.* The man stared around, scanning the room. He took a step, and then another step, and then he was standing in front of the mattress, facing away. *Now,* said Uncle.

Now. He kicked the mattress forward with his feet and slid down the wall behind it, throwing himself forward. He heard the thump and felt the impact as the other man's body was knocked forward, and he fell on that lump with all his weight. There was a cry, and he could see a head and one hand trying to extract itself from under the mattress. The hand still clutched a gun. Pulling the hammer from his belt, he hit the hand with it several times, as hard as he could. The man yelled and the gun went off again, shooting holes in boxes stacked on the shelving units. *Finish it,* said Uncle. Erlik took a deep breath and laid the hammer into the back of the protruding head. One, two, three, four, and then he felt the crunch and his arm sagged back.

You are a warrior, Uncle said as he struggled to his feet. *Now go be a healer. He is in there.* Erlik's hand unclenched on the hammer and it fell to the floor beside the mattress. Opening the door, he saw the tight knot of students gathered around someone lying on the floor. Their heads jerked up, faces full of fear, as he entered, and then the fear turned to amazement as they realized that it wasn't the gunman. *Yeah, just some weirdly dressed Asian guy, walking mysteriously out of the closet*, he thought to himself, his lip twisting, and then he said, "It's over. I killed him. Get out of here, all of you—get the paramedics." He crossed to the student lying on the floor, gasping and making small pathetic noises, and dropped to his knees.

His breath came in as he realized that the shooting victim was also Asian—in ordinary clothes, though, he realized. Shock of black hair sticking straight up, tears running from his eyes, lip clenched in his teeth. Bleeding from his leg, rather copiously. The other students were making for the door like rats from a sinking ship. Erlik took off the belt that was wrapped around the sash of his *del*, stripped the various bags off of it, and tried to loop it around the boy's thigh. The boy cried out and tried to stave him off, but Erlik grabbed his hands. "It's all right! I just have to tourniquet your leg before the paramedics come. I'll try not to hurt you, I promise."

"Is—is he—"

"He's gone," Erlik promised him. "I sent him to his ancestors. What's your name?" Give him something to focus on.

"Vang," he whispered. "Paj Vang."

Someone else might have given me their first name first, Erlik thought, one corner of his mouth quirking up. Vang was a common Hmong last name. "Listen to me, Paj," he said. "I'm not going to let anyone hurt you. I'm going to stay with you until the paramedics come to take you to the hospital. But you have to let me help stop the bleeding."

The boy nodded slowly, his eyes fixed on Erlik's, and moved his hands. Erlik got the belt around his thigh as gently as possible, although his hands were shaking and he fumbled the buckle.

When he pulled it tight, Paj cried out. "I'm sorry, I'm sorry," he said, but then had to yank it again to secure it. Paj moaned and his eyes rolled up. Erlik grabbed his hand and held it. "Paj, look at me. Stay with me. Stay awake, okay?" *Wish I knew a single word in Hmong.* "Talk to me about something. What's your major?"

The dark eyes flickered back open. "Math." His breath came in long gulps. "I'm a dork."

Enough of him still there to make a joke. Good. "I suck at math," Erlik said. "You're not a dork. Or at least no more than any Asian guy, huh?"

This got a small smile. "Who are you?" Paj asked.

"I'm Erlik. Erlik Solongo." While he kept the boy talking, his other hand roved about an inch above the wound. *Uncle, help me keep him from bleeding out. Spirits of the ancestors, spirits of the animals, raise my windhorse.*

"What are you doing?" Paj asked. *Damn, he noticed.*

Erlik sighed. "I'm a shaman. I'm trying to help keep you alive." His hand moved in the nine circles. "*Hurai, hurai, hurai.* Tenger of the four directions, bless us. *Bajat ayuki suuha. Manggalam.*" Then he looked up, and met Paj's wide eyes again.

At that moment, paramedics and police burst through the door. Erlik was elbowed aside and managed to move out of the way of their ministrations, but he couldn't move too far because Paj was still clinging to his hand with a deathgrip. The boy's face was too pale and his head began to loll. "Stay with me, Paj," Erlik said urgently. "Stay with me until they can get you out of here."

"Don't go," the boy whispered.

The paramedics were barking paramedic-jargon, and then a stretcher arrived. "I don't know if I can go with you to the hospital," Erlik began uncertainly, and eyed the nearest paramedic.

"You family?" he asked.

"No," Erlik said, and then thought better of it, but it was too late. *Likely he'd believe it—Asians all look alike to them. I should have said yes.* "I'm—I'm a friend."

"You can meet us at the hospital. Saint Mark's." And then Paj's hand was pulled out of his as they got the boy onto the stretcher, and his agonized eyes were Erlik's last sight as they rounded the corner. He looked up for the first time, then, and noticed the cops standing there. "You see who got him?" one of them asked.

Erlik's hand skidded on a bookbag as he tried to get up. A notebook fell out, labeled with the name Paj Vang, and he quickly scooped up both the bag and the book. "I did," he said. His fingerprints were on the hammer; there was no point in denying it. "And I'll tell you all about it, but right now, please, I need to go to St. Mark's hospital to see if Paj is going to be all right."

The cops moved a little closer. Erlik supposed that he did look a little odd, his long mane of hair come loose from its ponytail and flying all over the place, his embroidered *del* and bare feet, Paj's blood on his hands. "He's in good hands," said the police-woman next to the one who had first spoken. "I think you need to come down to the station and tell us what happened."

They kept him a good three hours, making him tell the story over and over. Fortunately, he'd had the length of the car ride to decide which details to leave out. *My name is Erlik Solongo. Yes, that's Mongolian. Yes, like Chinggis. No, not like Mongo's Barbecue Joint. Yes, I'm a student, here's my ID. I clean the labs twice a week, I was in the closet when he came in, I hid. Why was the window open? I thought about jumping out, thought better of it. I heard him talking on the phone to you guys. I heard him shoot Paj. He decided to check the closet, I climbed up on the mattress and knocked it down on him. His gun went off, fired a couple of rounds into Mr. Juma's storage. I hit him with the hammer, then I went out to tourniquet Paj's leg. That's when the paramedics came in.* He repeated it calmly, impassively, several times, and wrote it all down for them. Eventually, they let him go, and he walked a few blocks and got on a bus toward the hospital.

He was still shaking with the knowledge that he'd killed someone, killed him with his own hands. *You are a warrior,* Uncle had said, but mostly he felt like he was in shock. He had done the right thing, but there was no triumph to it, only a grim emptiness. He badly needed to know if Paj was all right. It would be one obvious good thing that had come of all this.

At the hospital, he blatantly lied about being Paj's family—he figured that the hospital staff would see his Asian features and buy it, and he was right. He hurried down the hall and pushed his way into the right room... and was confronted by Paj, laying in the hospital bed, and an older Asian couple sitting in chairs next to him. The woman clutched her purse with a deathgrip, and both of them stared at him as if he was a spectre appearing in the doorway. *Shit. Of course he'd have actual family here, I should have known. Damn.*

Paj's eyes lit up, and he began a sudden stream of what Erlik figured to be Hmong, which transfigured the faces of the older couple. He switched in midstream to English, saying, "I'm telling them that you are the man who saved my life."

Erlik smiled. "Well, actually, I expect that the paramedics saved your life," he said, spreading his hands in a no-big-deal gesture.

Those dark eyes were on him, intense, devouring. "You killed him. If you hadn't done that, I would have bled to death on the floor." Then the older couple were on him, clucking, patting his sleeve, smiling. He smiled and bowed to both of them, remembering to do the little wai bow with the hands together because they were from southeast Asia. They bowed back, keeping up the stream of chatter. Erlik nodded and kept smiling, which was the polite thing to do when you had no idea what was going on. *Even raised by assimilationists, I learned that.*

"I told them what you said—that you were a shaman," said Paj, sounding a little shyer. "But you're not Hmong, are you? And you're... young."

Erlik nodded. "You're right, I'm not Hmong. I'm a *buu*. That's Mongolian. And I'm... still learning. But you can tell them that my spirits got me in the right place, and helped me to do him in." He met Paj's glance, full-on, and the other youth blushed and looked away. "I brought your bookbag," he offered, holding it up. "I thought you might want it."

Paj translated everything, and the older man asked what was clearly a sharp question. His son hesitated, and then said, "They want to know if there is anything that they can do for you. In thanks."

Erlik was about to shake his head, but then he stopped. "Actually, yes, there is. I need to make offerings to my spirits, tonight or tomorrow, but I won't be getting any money for a few days. Normally I clean the labs for pocket money, but... well, crazed gunmen kind of killed my job today. Would your parents have any incense they could spare, or some vodka, or fruit? My spirits like those, and I should really thank them for both our lives." He said it calmly, but his palms were sweating. He wasn't sure if this would be considered rude, but he did need to make offerings. They'd gone out of their way for him, today.

Paj translated, and the couple lit up and chattered further. "They will be happy to bring you offerings for your spirits," he reported. "They will drive to Chinatown now and pick them up, if you are willing. They were going to bring me some dinner anyhow—I'm going to be held overnight and released," he said.

"Then I'll wait, and gladly," Erlik responded. "I wanted to talk to you anyway, see if you were all right,"

Paj blushed again. "They will bring us all dinner. If—if you'll stay—"

"Sure, I'll stay with you." He bowed to them again. "Mr. Vang. Mrs. Vang. How do you say thank you in Hmong?"

"*Ua koj thaug,*" said Paj. "Although it should be us who are thanking you."

There were a few more exchanges of bows, and then they left. Erlik pulled up a chair next to the bedridden boy, and asked, "How's the leg?"

"Well, they got the bullet out of it," Paj said. "It only went into the muscle tissue, missed the bone and the artery, so I was luckier than I could have been." His eyes were still devouring Erlik. "You meant what you said, about being a shaman, then? I wasn't sure if you were kidding around."

"No. I am a *buu*, or at least I am studying for it. I am *bagshagui*, which means that I don't have a human teacher around, and I'm learning straight from the spirits." He grinned wryly. "I'm also in school for Asian history and anthropology, because I have to do something in the real world as well. Besides, it might get me a grant to go to Mongolia."

"Well, you certainly impressed my parents. Good thinking, asking them to get offerings for the spirits, although you'd have been out of luck if they'd converted to Christianity. They believe you're for real now, at least." Paj smiled nervously.

"I didn't ask in order to impress your parents," Erlik said calmly, the smile vanishing. "I did it because I need the offerings. It's part of what keeps the wheels greased between me and my spirits." He paused. "Do you believe I'm real? That I'm serious?"

Paj hesitated again. "I believe you're serious. Whether I believe in all that traditional spirit stuff... I don't know. I've been trying to get away from that, as fast as I can. To be modern. The traditional ways aren't... good for me."

"Why not?" Erlik asked. "I mean, I don't know much at all about Hmong culture, and I'm not saying that there aren't plenty of customs that we could do without, but... that sounded to me like you meant it personally."

The youth in the bed turned his head away, and his voice was tight and angry. "I'm a disgrace to my family," he said. "When I was laying there on the floor, shot and bleeding out, do you know what I was thinking? That my family would be happier if I was dead. According to the old ways, I'm better off that way." His voice cracked, and then he went on, "And then you walked in like something out of some history book. My first thought, I kid you not, was that you were some spirit of the ancients, come to take me away to death. Except then you saved my life. And you're not a spirit."

"No," said Erlik. "I just work for them. And for what it's

worth, my parents are completely assimilated—and I'm a disgrace to my family, too." He smiled, and Paj let out a short, choking laugh in spite of himself. The moment lightened, and Erlik took a chance. "Of course, my own family disgrace is only halfway about the fact that I ran off to be some kind of superstitious juju-man. The other half of it is because I'm gay."

Dead silence fell between them. Erlik waited, thinking, *If he doesn't say something in another few seconds I'm going to go back to being dead polite, and maybe excuse myself and sit in the hall until the parents arrive with my schwag. Boy, am I stupid. Should have kept my big mouth shut.* And then, in a very small voice, Paj said, "So am I."

A rolling wave of warmth seemed to pass out from Erlik's heart to flow through his body, and he closed his eyes and smiled. *Ah, thank you, Uncle. Now I see.* "And your parents know, and they're angry because you won't be giving them grandchildren," he said. "I understand."

Paj turned back to look at him. "Yeah. I guess you would."

"Do you have a boyfriend?" Erlik asked, trying to keep his voice casual, as if it was some small-talk triviality, but Paj jerked in surprise.

"I—no, of course not," he said. "I've never even done anything. Except know. And say something about it, once. That was a mistake."

Erlik stood up and came over to him. "Honesty is never a mistake," he said, and took Paj's chin in his hand, and leaned over. He stopped there, two inches from Paj's face, and waited. If the youth had twisted away, or evaded his glance, he would have let go. Instead, Paj stared at him, breath coming hard, lips parting slightly, fear and desire in his eyes. That, Erlik realized, explained his intense stare. *Fear and desire.* He leaned over the rest of the way and sank his tongue into Paj's mouth.

His hand moved around to the back of Paj's neck and he held him firmly in place while devouring him. *This is what it's like when a man kisses you, boy. It's not gentle. See, it starts out gentle for a moment, and then* it's animal, crushing into you, taking you. Will you give back as good as you get, or will you take it passively? Either is fine with me, but it will tell me who you are. Ah, you yield to me, you don't even move your hands to encircle me. I see you now. I see you... and I will have you. Uncle sent you to me. He let go, abruptly, and smiled into Paj's gasping face. "You could have said no," he said, "if you didn't want it."

The other youth nodded, but didn't speak. Erlik suddenly realized that his hands were still stained with dried blood. "I should use your bathroom," he said softly, jerking his head at the small toilet room in the corner. "I've still got your blood on my hands."

Paj's breath came even harder. And that turns us both on, doesn't it? "Not just your hands," Paj whispered. "There's flecks of it in your hair, too."

Erlik's eyebrows went up. "You didn't spatter. So that must be...." His mouth twisted and he stood up. "I'll be right back."

After washing all the blood he could find off of hands, face, hair, and the shoulders of his *del*, he came back in and smiled at Paj, whose eyes devoured him again. Deliberately, he turned in a circle with his hands held out. "Look better?" he asked, "Good enough not to shock the parents?"

"I think my parents will love you," Paj said bitterly. "Even though you're not Hmong. They think a lot of our shamans."

"Good." Erlik's blunt statement brought Paj out of his downward spiral of self-loathing. "If they like me, they'll be fine with me befriending you. And you going off to hang out with me." He came back over to Paj's bedside. "Assuming that you like the idea, that is." One finger ran along Paj's cheek. With this small touch, I make you a little more mine. Every time I touch you, more of you will belong to me.

Paj looked like he was going to cry, but nodded. "When are your parents coming back?" Erlik asked. "How long do we have?"

"A couple of hours. It'll take them at least forty-five minutes to get there, then the shopping and waiting for takeout, then that much back." He shifted in the bed. "But it's not like I can go anywhere."

Erlik sat on the edge of the bed. "We don't need to go anywhere," he said. Then he lifted his leg and straddled Paj on the bed in one quick movement. He'd had years of horseback riding; that move came naturally. "I figured you might want to make up for lost time," he said, looking down at Paj's hospital-gown-clad figure in the bed. The young Hmong man cried out as he moved, and he added, "Is this hurting your leg?"

"Um, no, it's, um," and Paj blushed. Erlik felt the lump right under his balls and smiled, and wriggled his pelvis a little just to tease. Then he lay down on top of his prize, careful not to put any weight on the splinted leg, and began to kiss him again. This time the kisses moved in short order to the youth's neck, and then the johnny was pulled down to expose the shoulder which needed more nibbling, and then the covers were pulled aside to expose Paj's erection coiled in his underwear, and the underwear was eased off, and Erlik was forcing his tongue down Paj's throat again while one hand held the back of his neck and the other one wrung a quick muffled orgasm out of him.

He held his hand, with Paj's come on it, up to the youth's mouth. "Lick it off," he said. "If you're going to be with me, all come goes into you. Yours and mine. That's the first rule."

Paj swallowed. "Do I get to help make these rules?" he asked.

"No," said Erlik. "If you come with me, I'm in charge. But you'll have the ride of your life, and you'll never forget it." *Believe it. Please. Believe it.*

Paj parted his lips and docilely licked the come off of Erlik's hand. Then he said, "Yours too?"

"When I'm sure it's safe, yes. I'll go get tested at the clinic, so you can have a clean bill of results, and then we'll see."

"I don't need that. It's not important."

"It is important. It's a matter of my honor, and my honor is my windhorse. And if you're going to be with me, you need to stop being self-destructive." His own erection chafed against his trousers, and he pulled up the skirts of his *del* and pulled down his pants. "Have you ever sucked cock, Paj?"

He shook his head. "I told you, I've never done anything. Well, until now."

"Then you'll have to learn." Erlik dug in his pocket and came up with a condom, which he opened and rolled onto his cock. Paj watched in frightened fascination as Erlik moved forward until he was kneeling on either side of Paj's shoulders, and then brought the rubber-covered cock up to his mouth. "Open up," he said. "Just keep your lips and jaw loose, and let me fuck your mouth. If you start to choke, hold your breath and open up the back of your throat." He slid the end of his cock between Paj's lips, but didn't thrust in to the hilt. Instead, he moved the head of his cock in and out gently, letting the young Hmong man get used to the sensation. He glanced back over his shoulder and noticed that Paj was hard again. "Play with your cock while you suck mine," he ordered him. "It'll make your throat looser."

Paj obligingly began to rub his cock, and Erlik thrust just a little deeper. When Paj choked, he pulled back, let him breathe with a few shallow strokes, then went deep again. *This is training. You'll learn how to breathe when you can.* It was a rhythm, a dance, and Paj was learning quicker than he'd hoped. By the time he was ready to come, he could get his cock almost all the way down his throat, at least every few strokes. "Come," he gasped. "Come when I come. Do it!" He heard the slapping noise of Paj speeding up his strokes, then as the man's hips began to buck he buried his cock and held his head in place. Paj choked and wriggled, but he held him until he was done. Until they were both done.

Pulling out, he quickly rolled off the condom and tossed it into the trash, and then lay down next to the gasping, tear-streaked face that stared up at him. "You all right?" he asked. "If I was too hard on you, if that was awful, you tell me. Feedback is important." He took a tissue from the stand next to the hospital bed and wiped Paj's eyes.

The Hmong man sniffed. "No, no, that was... oh no, I've got it all over me." He looked, dismayed, at where he had come all over his belly. Erlik smiled, wiped it up with a finger, and tucked it gently into Paj's mouth. Paj sucked on his finger just a little, smiling around it, teary eyes and all. As Erlik removed his hand, he said, "I'd better clean up before my parents come back."

"You didn't answer," said Erlik gently but inexorably. "Was that too hard?"

Paj's mouth twisted up on one side. "It was hard. But it made me come like crazy. And—and if I practice, it won't be so hard, right?"

"Then we'd better practice more in the future. If you want that."

"Oh, yeah," he whispered. "I want it."

"Good," said Erlik. "Because I am so looking forward to fucking you."

He swallowed, and looked a little frightened, but not too much. *Good. I want you a little frightened, but not as much as you are turned on.* He fetched Paj a wet washcloth and helped him clean his face and belly and genitals, and cleaned his own. By the time Paj's family came back with dinner and spirit offerings, Erlik was sitting demurely by Paj's bedside discussing campus issues, and any remaining redness in Paj's eyes could be dismissed as a side effect of having been shot that morning. A nurse came in and administered more painkillers, and Paj quickly became sleepy; as his last act he talked his parents into driving Erlik back to the campus to pick up his bike.

That night Erlik lit one of the two veritable bales of incense that the Vangs had bought him, and poured out an entire bottle of vodka, and laid out half of the remaining Thai food for the spirits, and nearly two bags of oranges and mangoes. He knelt and thanked all of them profusely, but Uncle most of all. *Thank you, Uncle, for knowing what I needed. For delivering him into my hands. Thank you, thank you, thank you.*

Chapter Three

Online journal, May 20:

The first time I saw him, it was through a haze of pain. He walked up, spattered in blood, in that fancy embroidered coat, his long hair all over the place like a black wind. All right, I sound like a romantic idiot, but you have to understand that I was half out of my head with pain and shock and he really did look like that. Like something out of a movie. A Mongol warrior, come to kill me. Only he knelt down and held my hand, and kept me going. And he killed that man. It was all over the papers—the local reporters caught him on the way to school the next day, all done up in his traditional coat and his motorbike boots with his hair slicked up in that high tail on top of his head—I saw the pictures. Him leaning up against a tree, all cool and deadpan, like he killed crazed gunmen every day. Some of the news stories were respectful about him calling himself a buu, some of them made jokes about how he'd convinced himself that he was a shaman. He told them, the reporters, that it was his spirits who had helped him to get the guy.

I read all the articles to my parents, all the ones I could get my hands on. I wanted them to hear about him, to admire him, to be angry—as I knew they would be—at the reporters' snide dismissal of his traditional religion. I wanted them to think well of him. I also wanted to be the one to read them the stories because there were things I wanted to censor. Like when he told the reporters that he was gay.

"Why did you do that?" I asked him wildly when he showed up the next day. He just smiled at me and told me that he didn't have to answer to any parents any more, and anyhow things weren't going to change unless someone did something. And this was one thing he could do. And I looked into his eyes while he said that. They were so intense.

He's brave. Really brave. He wants something, and he just does it. I'm not brave. What's he going to think when he finds out what kind of a coward I am?

It's so funny, really. I was fixated on white guys. I was going to find a white American boyfriend, someone tall with big muscles and blond hair who was absolutely modern, who would help me to escape my traditional culture and never look back. That's what I wanted. That's what I looked at in magazines. That's what I beat off to. And then this Mongolian guy with the Chinese face, and while I've never actually stood up in his presence I think he's an inch or so shorter than me, and he dresses halfway in traditional clothing and says he's a frigging shaman, how much more backward can you get? He's the absolute opposite of what I was looking for.

And yet he's sitting there telling me why it's important to be out as gay. And yet he got on top of me and put his cock in my mouth. Two days in a row, now. He kissed me and bit me and turned me into fucking jello. He took me like Genghis Khan fucking took a city, and I just lay there and came, because I want him so fucking much. Because it's like a fairy tale—my Mongol warrior who came out of the mists of the pasts and plundered my virgin ass.

Well, okay, he hasn't touched my virgin ass yet, because I'm in the hospital with my leg in a splint, and it isn't practical. But he's told me, in graphic detail, that he intends to do it. He told me while his long hair fell all around me like a veil, shutting out the world. Like a fucking fairy tale. And then he said, "Of course, you can always say no." Could I? Somehow that would feel like rejecting the fairy godmother's gift. I kind of feel like I'd be an idiot to do that. Besides, he saved my life. Doesn't that kind of mean that it's his now?

I want him so bad my hands are shaking, typing this on my

laptop. Fortunately this journal entry is locked to everyone. What the fuck would I do if my sister found it and read it to my parents? They love him. They wouldn't love him so much if they knew I was sucking his cock. Is it just gratitude because of what he did? Save the princess and then she's yours, only in a gay way? No, what's motivating my cock every time I think of him is not gratitude. Is it that I imprinted on him, in a moment of pain and vulnerability? Is it that he's just the first man who ever grabbed my dick and made me come? I don't know, but I'm not sure that I could say no to him. To anything he wanted. At all.

And that is fucking scary. And that is so, so very hot.

It was a few days before Erlik could get over to see Paj at his home. Those days were spent dodging reporters, or at least leaving a trail that led away from where he actually lived. He had no wish to advertise that he lived in a tent in an asphalted back yard and couldn't afford a roof over his head, or a cell phone. He told them that his number was private and that he was only available for interviews during lunch hour at school. When they pressured him for more, he gave them the inscrutable Asian stare for as long as necessary, and they backed off.

One really good thing came of it, though. One of the mothers of the students in that room, the students who had run for the door while he stayed with Paj, had come over personally to give him her thanks. It was a day when his bicycle had broken, and he'd looked dismally at the rain and said that he'd stay in the library until it was over. He'd made a small comment about how his pony was lame, and she'd laughed. Then she'd called up later and asked if he wanted her son's motorcycle, because her son had abandoned it when he'd gone off to school in another state, and he had another one now. And it was just sitting there gathering dust until she could get around to selling it, and... the next day he signed the papers for the Suzuki and climbed aboard a real horse.

He named her Arza after the traditional drink of Mongolia— fermented mare's milk—and when he went to pick Paj up, it was on his new mare's back. It would be a few days before he could actually get his motorcycle license, but he'd asked the spirits to make sure that no one would stop him before that time.

Paj was on crutches, which he lashed crosswise to the seat, and helped the other man onto the part of the seat behind them, carefully propping his leg out. "I'll go slow," he promised. "It'll be all right." Paj looked dubious, but when he straddled his mare and started her, he felt arms go around him tightly, and a head lean ever so slightly on his shoulder. It was dark out, so no one could see that closely, and they rolled off down the street.

Even so, he was as nervous as ever—and perhaps more so— when he unlocked the gate that surrounded his tent. It was always hard, bringing people in here. They usually wouldn't understand. With Paj, things were so new, so fragile... he was still unsure as to whether he wanted to keep impressing him, blowing him away, until he was thoroughly bound, and then reveal his inner self—or whether it was better just to be honest from the begin- ning. *Honest about Eric Chang from Fresno? Not yet.* He helped Paj into the darkness of the tent and got him settled on the cot, and then set about lighting candles. When the place was lit up, he sat down next to him and waited, for once unsure of what to say.

Paj looked around, taking everything in. "What are those?" he asked, indicating the painted cloths on the ceiling.

"Spirits that I work with, or that I honor. I painted them myself." *On pieces of old trashpicked sheets.*

"And the altar? That's where you do your... rituals?"

Erlik sighed. "Think of me as a professional, Paji. That's my worktable. It's as if I was a machinist—that would be my table of fancy tools. This is what I do. The degree, that's just something to assist this. What you see is my life. Can you live with that? With me?" When the young man didn't answer, his brow furrowed, he added, "I listen to Garbage, and Blues Traveler, and Nine Inch Nails. I have a boom box under the bed. I go to leather bars. I do live in the twenty-first century in America. I just happen to have a job that's kind of... retro."

Paj choked with laughter. "Retro! That's one way to put it." His voice softened. "Paji?"

"It's how I think of you. I'll stop, if you like."

The young man paused, then shook his head. "It's all right." He seemed to draw into himself. *Must stop that.* Erlik put a hand under his chin and turned his face around.

"I want you," he said. "But I want more than just to fuck you. I want to make you proud of what we are. I want to show you how good it can be." With his other hand, he smoothed back the shock of black hair that fell over Paj's eyes. "Trust me to take you there?"

Paj nodded, eyes wide. "Say it," commanded Erlik.

"I trust you," he whispered.

Erlik smiled at him, and then stood up and began to shuck his clothing. Coat, sash, T-shirt and pants, underwear and boots and socks. He had the strong feeling that Paj had never had the chance to look at a naked man up close and actually have the chance to touch him, and that his usual top-distance would be counterproductive here. He stood in front of the startled young man, his cock on a level with Paj's face. "Touch me," he said. "Go ahead, it's all right. If you do something wrong, I'll redirect you."

A flash of fear crossed Paj's face, but then he reached out and slid a hand down Erlik's thigh. A trembling hand. Erlik smiled down at him. *No, I don't need to be the one with clothes on to be in charge.* Another hand joined the first, moving up to his ribcage and across his stomach, down his thighs again, then—hesitantly—around to the back where they cupped the cheeks of his ass. Then back to his thigh, and Erlik realized that Paj was touching his tattoos. There were several of them, spirit-figures running across his body. He turned around, let Paj see the ones on his back, although he couldn't reach them from his sitting position. Paj stroked his ass some more, and then he felt a small kiss on each buttock. "Yes," he said. "Do that again." More kisses followed. Erlik moaned, feeling his cock harden. He reached back and spread his ass cheeks, showing Paj his asshole, and heard the other man's breath draw in. Then he turned back around to face him.

"Someday you'll kiss me there," he said, and slid his hand into Paj's hair, tightening, shaking his head slightly. "Now touch me here." He indicated his stiffening cock. Paj stroked him, cupped his balls with the same gentle hesitant touch he'd used to cup his ass, then slid the cock into his mouth. For one moment Erlik sank, moaning, into the warm wetness, then he gasped and pulled Paj off him by the hair. "Not so fast, boy," he said. "I know you're dying to suck me bareback, but you don't get to do that just yet. Be patient. We're going to do things right." *If nothing else, it will get you used to a safe process before you hurtle yourself into an unsafe situation with someone else. Maybe it's a good thing that you haven't had the chance to run around being a slut.*

The young man's face was woeful, and Erlik had to laugh and kiss him. "My turn," he said, and tumbled Paj back onto the cot. It took longer to get his leg propped and his clothes off, and then Erlik explored his body greedily, hungrily, possessively. *Every time I touch you, more of you will belong to me.* He spat on Paj's cock and jerked it off, but the saliva wasn't enough for good friction. "Hold on a second," he said, and grabbed the lube from under the bed. With a handful of that, his hand slid along that long, thin cock without a hitch, and the other man threw his head back with a guttural noise and squirmed.

Erlik waited until he was half out of his head and then stopped, grabbing a towel and wiping his hand off. Paj's eyes came open with a wounded-puppy look. "Not yet," Erlik said. "Don't worry, you'll get off, but I want to reposition you first. And that leg is going to be a bit of a problem. But it's all right, I know what we can do."

It took nearly half an hour—during which, Erlik was pleased to note, Paj still kept most of an erection—to get him propped face down with his hips comfortably elevated on pillows. There seemed to be no way to prop his leg comfortably in that position, so Erlik resorted to moving it around in the air until Paj proclaimed it comfortable, and then rigging some rope to the struts of the *ger* above to hold it suspended in place. The other end of the ropes were tied around Paj's chest, so that—as Erlik explained—he wouldn't be pulling against the ropes around his wounded leg, but would move all of a piece when he was jostled. He demonstrated this by grabbing Paj's cock again; the young man jerked, but his whole torso moved together. *What a nice excuse for your first bondage.* "Put your own hand on your cock," Erlik told him. "Start jerking it off, but don't come till I tell you." Then he pulled a rubber glove out from the bag under his bed and snapped it onto his hand. His rope-bound partner flinched at the sound, but Erlik put his bare hand gently on the young man's ass and stroked it. Paj calmed immediately, and Erlik put more lube on his fingers and, very slowly, inserted one of them in Paj's asshole.

The young man moaned audibly and jerked his cock faster. "Relax," Erlik said. "Open up for me. Let me in. You want me, your body wants me." He kept his voice a low monotone, comforting but hypnotic, or at least he hoped it would be. "This is going to feel really good, once we get through the gate. I need to you relax and help me get there." Two fingers, shallow, then in past the knuckles. "You are so beautiful, lying here like this. I fucking love your ass. I want your ass so much." Three fingers now. Paj's hand stilled on his cock, moved away; its hardness throbbed against the pile of pillows. Erlik had wanted him to keep himself aroused, but apparently the ass-stretching was doing that all of its own accord. Figuring that he'd better get in soon, he fumbled a condom onto his own cock with his other hand—*damn, should have done this before I started*—and then, as deftly as he could, slid his fingers out and his cock in.

Even though Erlik's fingers had opened him up, Paj still cried out when the head of Erlik's cock passed his sphincter. Erlik knew what that was about; it was the shock of the moment, of realizing that you'd actually done it, you were actually there in the moment with someone's dick up your ass, and any pretensions of being only in it for the blowjobs was now completely exploded. You were a fucking faggot being sodomized, and there was nothing for it but to accept yourself and enjoy it, because it was too late now.

He started moving slowly, both to get Paj used to it and to keep from jostling his suspended leg too much. Paj was silent at first; Erlik went to reach under him and grab his cock, but found the other man's hand in the way. "Please," Paj gasped. "It's taking everything I have not to come. If you touch me, I'll—"

Erlik pulled his hand back with a little puff of laughter. "Then I'm going to fuck you hard," he said, "and you go ahead and come whenever you like." He wrapped his arms around Paj from behind and started to pound into his ass. He'd thought that he was far away from an orgasm, but it came on him like a sudden storm. He heard himself crying out gutturally, and Paj gasping, "Yes, yes, yes," and Paj's asshole clamping down on his emptying cock like a vise. Then he had to roll off quickly so as not to put pressure on Paj's suspended leg, which put him next to the bound boy on the cot, looking up at his sweaty, contorted face and damp hair. Eyes wide, they gasped together for a moment, and then Paj leaned down and, for the first time, kissed him back.

It startled him, and he made a little sound of surprise, then allowed himself to relax into the kiss. One hand clamped the back of Paj's neck as a small reminder of his dominance, but he let the other man hesitantly probe his mouth. As they pulled away, Paj said, "Thank you."

Erlik smiled up at him. "Thank you, sir," he said.

Paj blinked, and his mouth moved soundlessly. Erlik held his breath. This was the moment—was he going to accept authority, or rebel? Yes, he was partially tied up and had just been thoroughly fucked for the first time, but a rebellious spirit would still be able to pull back and deny it, make a joke of it, something. Erlik would have. Paj looked into space for a moment, and then ducked his head and said, "Thank you, sir."

Jackpot. He slid his hand into Paj's black shock of hair and gripped it. "You see?" he said. "You see how good it can be?"

The sides of Paj's lips curled up. "Yeah," he said quietly.

"It can be even better. This was just the first time. What we are is beautiful. You are beautiful. Don't forget that." He shook Paj's head one last time and then let go. "Let me get you out of that. And cleaned up. And rolled over. And maybe even dressed again."

Paj snorted, and then sobered. "Not dressed just yet. Please? I want to—" He broke off shyly.

"You want body contact," Erlik said. "You want your naked body in the arms of another naked man." He watched Paj flush. "There's no shame in that, Paji. You're gay." He quickly worked the knots loose, lowered Paj's leg and levered him over, and then slid in next to him. "Luckily there's another naked fag right here," he said, and was gratified to hear a laugh.

Later, after cleaning up and carefully getting Paj and his crutches onto the bike, they stopped at a diner for food. "You probably eat traditionally at home," Erlik said. "Which do you prefer?"

Paj shrugged. "Traditional food usually tastes better, but there's something to be said for the... directness of American junk food. It's sort of primal. And artificial, all at the same time. Fake primal. That doesn't sound right, does it?" He wrinkled his brow. *You second-guess yourself all the time, don't you?* Erlik thought.

"Have you ever had really good Western food?" he asked. "I mean high-ticket Italian, or French, or something like that? Not just diners or fast food."

Paj shook his head. "My parents don't want to spend their money on expensive restaurants when they can make food at home for way less." His voice took on an unconscious cadence that suggested a remembered parental lecture. "And since I went to college last September, it's just been cafeteria food on my meal plan."

Erlik smiled. *I'll have to save some money and see if I can take us both out.*

"It's more subtle," he said. "And worth experiencing. Not all Western food is like naïve art. Just the food of poor people."

"Culinarily impoverished," said Paj.

"I've got a friend who calls it culinary illiteracy," Erlik commented. They were silent for a minute, working on their fries, and then he asked, "So now we're out of the dark and sitting in public, if—"—he looked around quickly—"—we're out of earshot. How do you feel about what we did tonight?"

Paj's eyes widened and he cringed. "You really want to talk about it now? Here?"

Erlik met his eyes evenly. "Who am I going to be to you, Paj? I understand that we have to be discreet around your family, for now. But what about the campus? Do your parents have friends there? What about in strange places where no one knows us? Are we stealth everywhere? Can I take you into a gay bar? Can I drive you there on my bike? What are you willing to learn to be comfortable with?" He deliberately phrased it that way, to drive his point home.

He could see the young man swallow and stare at his food. "I need some time to get used to this," he said in a small voice.

Erlik shrugged. "Fair enough. But I expect answers to those questions, at some point. I'll ask again in two weeks." *Two weeks of taking you. We'll see how that affects your answers.* "Let me ask you this, at least. How do you see your future? Ideally, I mean. If you could have anything."

"I wanted to get through school. Leave home. Move far away from my family. Find a boyfriend."

"And?"

"I... hadn't thought past that. I figured I'd do whatever work paid." He ducked his head. "I'm not very ambitious."

"So if you'd been a girl you'd be looking to be a housewife? Looking for your MRS degree?" He said it playfully, but Paj still cringed. "Fine. Let me tell you what I want. I want to finish my bachelor's—I graduate in June—and then go to grad school, get the MS so that I can get grants. I want to travel and research and write about it for a few years. I want to buy land, big enough so that I can have horses."

Paj blinked. "Horses?"

"I love horses. I work part-time in the campus stables, I told you that. Horses are expensive, so I figure I'd probably live with other people, have them pay part of their rent in cleaning stables and exercising horses when I'm traveling. Do you ride?"

He shook his head. "I've never even been near a horse."

"I'll have to take you out trail riding, when your leg's healed. Most important, though, I'll be doing my shamanic work. It will always come first in my life. Think of it like being with someone who is studying to be a trauma surgeon. Their work isn't going to be unobtrusive; it'll probably rule the household." He paused. "And I want a companion while I'm doing all this—someone who can be public and proud to be with me when we're in this country, and discreet when we're overseas in places where they wouldn't understand. Someone who knows that my work comes first, and who wants to support that."

Paj kept his eyes on his dish. "Do you actually... you know, see people? Like the shaman my parents go to, for good luck scrolls and such?"

"Yes, I see clients. Actually, since that newspaper article, I've been getting a lot more calls. Next week is booked solid. Mostly they're white and they want readings. It'll probably trickle off as soon as my five minutes of fame are over." *And I'll take as much as I can get in the meantime.*

"And you go to gay bars?" Paj asked. "Dressed like that? Or do you change into, you know, normal clothes?"

Erlik smiled. "These are my normal clothes. Yes, I go dressed just like this. Of course, I tend to go to leather bars, and there are people dressed a lot stranger than me sometimes."

Paj's eyes snapped up at the word leather. "And you like...." He trailed off.

"I like all kinds of things." Erlik popped another fry into his mouth. "I like cute guys. I like tying them up, but only if they consent to it. I like hurting them, but only if they're into it. I'm not a rapist, I'm a gourmand." He ate another fry, with a flourish, and a chuckle escaped Paj in spite of himself. "I like being in charge," he said, softer. "But I'm not interested in being an evil dictator. I like to think of myself as a good leader, and I learn from my mistakes. I want to be worth following."

The other man was silent for a moment, and then asked, even more hesitantly, "The places that you go, the leather bars... are all the guys there, um, are they all only into doing it if you, um, want it?"

Erlik's eyebrows went up. "You mean, are they full of big mean daddies out to rape the ass of anyone who walks in and can't fight them off? Honey, if that was the case I'd have already killed two or three of them. No, there are a few jerks that need to be fended off, but the rule is consent. Nobody's ever gotten raped there that I know of. I'm not including the ones who wanted that, of course." He tilted his head to the side and narrowed his eyes at Paj. "I'd protect you, of course, if that's what you're asking. No one would fucking touch you except me. And that's a promise I can definitely make." He let his voice settle into a hard edge, and noticed Paj's eyes widen, just a little bit.

"You'd protect me," he said. "Like I was your property."

Bingo. "Like I was responsible for you," Erlik said calmly. "Which I would be. I mean, I just took your fucking virginity, that means something to me." Paj blushed. "I'm not trying to make out like you're a weakling—"

Paj clenched his fists. "Why not? I am a weakling, a faggot weakling. I can't even—" He broke off as Erlik reached over and took both his hands, uncurling the fingers and holding them, hard. He willed Paj to look up, and he did, finally.

"Then borrow my strength," Erlik said. "It's here for you."

Chapter Four

Borrow my strength, he said. Then he took me home, and just before he walked me inside he pulled me behind the bushes and pressed me up against the wall, and kissed me so hard that it was an effort not walking into my parents' house with an erection. I couldn't look them in the eye, either, not without flashing back to a sudden image of hanging there being fucked up the ass. I knew that would show on my face, so I mumbled something about being tired and went to bed. My mother scolded Erlik half-heartedly about keeping me out until I was exhausted, which I translated, and he bowed to her and apologized. But he didn't say that he wouldn't do it again.

The last thing he said to me before walking me inside was "I don't want you to come until you're alone with me again. But I won't make you do it. I want you to choose that, for me. It's up to you." So here I am, having jerked off four times in the past two days, and abandoned the project in the middle each time. It's not that I'm not desperately horny, especially every time I clench my ass and remember what it was like. But I keep thinking about saving it for him, and that always seems like it would be hotter, and I stop. I'm going to die from blueballs if this goes on, which it looks like it will, because he's got clients all this week. "I have to make a living," he said. "I'm paying for all this myself."

That's the one place I've seen a chink in his armor, actually. He's a little prickly about the fact that he lives in a tent in somebody's storage yard, and scrapes for every cent. I saw him scan his wallet carefully when we walked into the diner, and saw the flash of relief, and then the flicker of shame, when I told him I would buy my own meal. *I've been poor,* I want to say to him, my family doesn't have a lot, we scrape to pay the electric bill sometimes. My parents aren't paying for my college either; the state is. But I don't want to prod that point too much. It can't be much of a living, being a shaman in this day and age. As far as I can tell, he doesn't cater to a traditional community, either. There is something entirely alone about it. I'm both fascinated to pry into his life, and scared of it. I don't want to have to believe some of the things he says.

And again, my mind is going back to my cock. All I can think of is going ass-up for him again. I've been walking around the house looking at small narrow cylindrical things like handles and bottles, and thinking, That would fit up my ass. I was always kind of turned off by the idea before this week, but now that I've done it, all I can think of is doing it again. Except that as horny as I am, I'm afraid that sliding something into my ass would make me shoot off, and I'm saving myself for Erlik. Isn't that stupid? I'm fucking saving my come for some guy.

Except that the thing I really want up my ass is his cock. Anything else would be a let-down. I want to feel his balls slapping against mine. I want to feel his body against my back, his tight wiry arms around me. I want him to take me, again.

I'm kind of ashamed at how much I like being taken. Will I ever be able to give, to open up and reciprocate? Would he want that? There's kind of no point in asking him, since I'm not ready to do it anyway. He can tell that I'm ashamed of it, and that I want it, and that I'm ashamed about how much I want it. He's made little comments to that effect, and they are always followed up by something about how I'll feel better about it all when I'm used to it. Used to being gay, I guess. Only it's not the being gay part that's the worst. It's being a bottom, to use his word. Doesn't that mean I'm no better than a woman? I don't want to be a woman, though. I just want to be with him.

He had a little tear in his sleeve, and for a second I wanted to mend it. Except that I've never sewed anything in my life. Isn't that stupid? He can sew, of course; he sews all his clothes on a friend's machine and he doesn't seem to think it makes him any less masculine. "Silly sexist stuff," he tells me. Chiding me for being old-fashioned while he stands there in his getup and gives half his leftover lo mein to the figures on his altar.

I asked him what makes him think that he can just pick and choose. He looked at me for a long minute, and then said something about how he asks the spirits what sort of cultural customs it's important for him to keep, and which ones they don't care about, and he goes from there. I asked him how that was supposed to be of relevance to me, since I couldn't hear his damn spirits, they couldn't talk to me or anyone else I knew. He said, "That's kind of the point of having shamans."

Fuck this. I can't just sit here and wait for him to tell me to come. I cannot be this pathetic. I am going to go stick a handle up my ass now.

Fuck. Stuck a handle up my ass. It felt so good that I went and got a shampoo bottle. As soon as I got it up there, I came without touching my cock. I was thinking about how much easier it would be for Erlik if I was stretching my ass open between dates, and I came. Fuck.

Chapter Five

It was almost a week before Erlik got to see Paj again, but the clients were coming thick and fast, and for once his wallet felt flush. He was able to buy more fabric for clothing, and stock up his food larder—actually buying a second cooler—and pick up a few extras, and buy used copies of next semester's books ahead of time from people who'd dropped out of the courses midway. There was no telling if he'd have enough book money when the time came, and anyway this meant that he could study up. He kept a cheerful stream of emails going to the youth, telling himself that he needed to make a living while it lasted. Meanwhile, his cock stirred every time he thought about Paj. He didn't jerk off, though. He wanted to save his first come for Paj's mouth, and have enough left to take his ass a couple of times. He knew from experience that saving it up as long as he could stand it was the best method for that.

He did take his frustrations out on Dali's back, though. Dali was a street kid, a friend of his who came around every couple of months to find a place to crash and get a beating from a safe top. Dali was very respectful to him, treated him like a holy man, and he always read for the kid for free. It was never good news, but he knew better to exhort him to get off smack and the streets. Instead he bruised up the kid's emaciated back with teeth-gritted intensity, and didn't take his pants off. He never fucked Dali anyway; it would be too dangerous, considering his history. Dali fell asleep on a pile of sheepskin on the floor and was gone by the time Erlik woke up in the morning.

He came for Paj on his bike again, and was gratified to be able to take him to a real restaurant with fine Italian food. Afterwards, they went back to his tent and Paj sat down on the edge of the bed. He seemed to be trying to make himself talk, so instead of immediately hitting on him, Erlik summoned all his willpower and sat down quietly next to him.

"I guess I should tell you that I didn't stay celibate for you," Paj said, as if he expected to be berated for it.

Erlik's mouth twisted, but he bit his tongue and pushed the feeling away. "I told you that it was your choice," he said. "I meant that." He kept his voice light and gentle, but his nails dug into his palms.

Paj's shoulders hunched over, as if still expecting the blow. His voice came in short, choppy waves. "I wanted to. And then I thought that it was stupid. And then I wanted something up my ass. And then I was angry at you for making me want something up my ass. And then somehow I got this idea that sticking something up my ass without you there would be... I don't know, some way to assert my independence or something. Except all that I could think of while I was shoving a shampoo bottle up my ass was whether you'd be pleased if I stretched out my ass for your cock. And that made me come. And then I realized I was the biggest idiot in the world."

Erlik spread one hand in a throwaway gesture. "Maybe it was too soon. I am sorry. I didn't mean to send you into an emotional tailspin."

Paj took a deep breath. "And then I stopped trying to jerk off since then, and I saved what was left for you." *Please don't make me wait too long*, hung in the air between them.

As before, Erlik stood up silently and began to strip off his clothes. He stood naked in front of Paj, ripped a condom out of its package, and rolled it on to his rapidly stiffening cock, inches from Paj's face. "If you want me," he said, "show me. Show me now."

Paj grabbed him by the hips and sank his mouth down on his cock. Erlik gasped in spite of himself, and then took hold of Paj's head, fucking his face, first gently and then harder. The boy choked, tears running from his eyes, and Erlik spoke to him in a low quick voice. "Yes, that's right. Fucking choke on my cock. Gag yourself on it and then shove it back in. Go ahead and choke, it's hot. I want it to be hot for you too. You're sexy, all covered in tears and snot, gagging on my cock. I want to feel the back of your throat, that's right. Hold your breath now, I'm shoving it all the way in. How long can you take it? Good boy. Good boy. Now breathe. Now open your throat again, you little fucker." His voice got hoarser and rougher, but he watched Paj like a hawk for the first sign of pulling away for more than a breath, of having had enough. "Let me fuck your face now. Be my fuckhole, that's right. Little cocksucker. That's right, grab my ass. Shove that cock deep into your throat. I can see how hard you are, in your pants. Take one hand and undo them, don't stop sucking, just free your cock. Don't fucking rub it, get your hand off it now. Put it back on my ass. I just want to see your hard cock while you're choking on mine. I'm going to fuck your face really hard now, I'm going to come down your throat." He grabbed Paj's head and threw his own head back, trailing off in a roaring grunt. The hands clenched on his buttocks, pulling them aside and exposing his asshole to the air as he came.

Gasping, he peeled off the condom and handed Paj the box of tissues to wipe down his wet, reddened face. "Oh, man," he said. "I really needed that." He grinned down at Paj. "You may not have saved yourself for this, but I did," he said.

A brief look of shock crossed the other man's face, and before it could turn to anything more ambivalent, Erlik leaned down and kissed him, and licked up the remaining tears. "Let's get you undressed," he said. "And then maybe you'd like to make my cock hard again, so that you can dance on it?"

Paj was open-mouthed, loose-lipped, breathing heavily. He raised his eyes to Erlik, wide and black. "Dancing," he whispered. "Is that what it is?"

"It can be," Erlik said. "Shall I tie you in place again?"

"...Yes."

"Shall I tie you up more than I did before?"

"...Yes."

"Good choice," he said, as if it he was a waiter taking a wine order. Paj's clothing came off, and the ropes came out, and soon he had him face down and hanging comfortably once more. This time however, he tied Paj's free ankle to the corner of the bed, and then gently brought the youth's wrists behind him and secured them. His immediate next move was to lubricate his hand and run it down Paj's cock—*it's important, the first time that someone has their hands tied, to touch their junk as quickly as possible. That way they get to struggle a little, just like he's doing now, and then relax into how erotic it is to be restrained.* "Don't worry," he whispered in Paj's ear. "I won't let you come until I've fucked you."

Reluctantly he separated himself from his lover's cock and moved over so that his own cock was right next to Paj's face. It was already half-hard again, and he tapped it against Paj's cheek, which got a slight giggle. "Come on," he said. "You want this up your ass—I know you do—so get it hard and wet again." Paj turned his head and Erlik tucked the cock almost tenderly into his mouth, letting him suckle on it until it was hard enough to penetrate. While Paj was working away, he got out lube and slowly worked his fingers into the man's asshole, which clenched a bit at first but then finally yielded.

When he got himself behind Paj and slowly sank into his ass, the young Hmong man's moan was entirely worth it. Erlik moved back and forth a little just to get him used to it, and then said, "What a good boy, to open up your ass for me. I think I want you to keep doing that, making yourself into a good little buttwhore for me." Paj made an even louder sound at that point, somewhere between a moan and a cry, but he pushed himself harder onto Erlik's cock with the one knee that was still on the bed. *Yes, you want it, but you're still scared of it. That's all right.* You'll come around. Erlik grabbed his hips and began to fuck him in earnest, and then it was just a wild fuck with the rhythm of horses pounding down the plains. At some point Paj came, crying out, and Erlik considered stopping as the other man's ass shrank down around his cock, and then decided against it and kept going until his own come. Paj was hanging, sobbing, in the ropes when he pulled out, but it wasn't the kind of sobbing that meant trauma. Erlik had seen that kind before. This was the kind that made him return Erlik's kiss with extra passion. *I've got you, boy. You may not know it yet, but I've got you.*

After ropes and condoms had been removed, they lay together quietly in the bed until Erlik spoke up. "I meant what I said," he remarked. "I'm not going to ask you to forgo orgasm while you're not with me. I want you to come. I want you to come a lot, actually. I just want to be in charge of how it's done. We can start with the rule that you don't come unless there is something in your ass, stretching you open."

Paj drew in his breath, paused, and then nodded against Erlik's chest. His hips moved against the shaman's thigh. "Yeah, that turns you on, doesn't it? I know it does, you don't have to say it. Second rule: if you want to come a second time during the day, you have to find something bigger and put it in."

He could feel Paj smile against his chest. "Is there a third rule, for a third time?" he asked.

"No," said Erlik. "The third rule is that you have to be thinking about me."

Paj froze, and then breathed spastically. "Anything about you?"

"Anything. Well, okay, I'd prefer that you didn't jerk off to the idea of me being drawn and quartered. But still." He paused. "And you have to say my name when you come. If only in a whisper."

Paj lifted his head a little to look at Erlik. "Are these rules all my choice to obey as well?" he asked.

"Of course." Erlik said calmly, hoping that Paj wouldn't feel his heart rate speed up. "I can't exactly force you to do anything, you know."

"You mean that you can't call your spirits to come enchant me, make me into your obedient robot?" Paj asked teasingly, but there was tension behind his voice.

As always, Erlik was forced to answer honestly when it was about the spirits. He often hated that this was the case, but they always made him do it anyway. "I think that they would just mock me for not being able to inspire you to do it of your own free will," he said.

The young Hmong man was silent for another few minutes, and then he said, "Why did you hold it—you know—for me?"

"Because you're worth it," Erlik said. His hand wandered down to Paj's balls, idly cupping them, putting his finger and thumb around the top of the ballsack to feel them bulge out, then letting go and cupping them again. Paj gasped and moved his hips again, involuntarily. Erlik just smiled, but inside his heart was racing.

Chapter Six

Online journal, June 19:

We went to the stables today, to celebrate me getting financial aid for summer classes. Can I just say that I did not want to spend my summer racking up more credits? This was not what I had in mind. I figured I'd spend the entirety of my summer lounging around watching TV, or, hey, how about getting fucked? Well, okay, I can't exactly complain about not getting fucked. I guess I just had this idea that we'd spend all our time together. But no, Erlik is taking summer classes because they're cheaper and he can get through grad school quicker if he does at least two classes in the summer, and he's making me take them to get myself to my B.S. quicker. So Calc 4 instead of beach time. He did all the forms and got financial aid for both of us, without even talking to me about it. "Here, sign this." I didn't know how to say no.

I figured the horseback riding—which I'd been dreading—was really a celebration that the grant and the loan for his M.S. had come through, but I also figured I wouldn't say that either. The campus stables were on the far side, up next to the state woods with all the trails, and I'd never been over there. When I think of this morning, I think of dust, the dusty ground I kicked up next to the fake split-rail fence while he went into the manure-smelling barn to find us horses. His favorite one, and something bombproof for me. I didn't want to go in—it was bad enough that I was going to have to get on the back of some large smelly animal and ride around, I didn't need to be surrounded by them and their odor. I enjoyed the feeling of the sun on my shoulders and the fact that I could kick around in the dust on two legs now. The cast was off and while I was still limping, I had healed up. There was still a big red puckered scar on my leg where I'd been shot, though.

Then I heard hoofbeats and a whicker behind me, and I turned around, and there he was riding out of the barn, limned by the sunlight. He was wearing his new dark green *del* and leading another horse by the reins, his hair all slicked up on top of his head in that long ponytail to get it out of the way. His own horse was apparently walking unguided, or maybe he was guiding it with his legs, I couldn't tell. All I know was that my heart leaped in my chest and then fell down into a puddle of melted ice cream. He really did look like a Mongol warrior, riding out of the desert; all he needed was archery equipment strapped to his back. I just gaped stupidly and then realized that I had a sudden erection.

I swear, this is so stupid. My head wants a big blond white guy and my dick wants a little Asian guy. Am I ever going to be able to bridge that gap between them?

Anyway, he stopped and squinted down at me, and then hopped off that horse with—I realized—the same motion that he hops off me when he's straddling me. That thought made me flush, too. "Come on up," he said. "I'll give you a lift. Don't worry, Heather's a good old mare, she's used to beginners. She's a patient lady and she's not going to dump you off just because you do something wrong."

He knelt in the dirt—I almost wanted to tell him not to do that, you'll get your new *del* all dirty—and made a cage of his hands to boost my heel up. Even so, it took a couple of tries. Then he stood, brushed off his split skirts, swung back up onto that horse like it was nothing, grabbed the reins of my unmoving mare, and was off. "Think of your spine as a piece of string hanging from the sky," he told me cheerfully, "and your butt is the weight at the bottom of the string. It's going to swing back and forth with the horse's motion, but you're going to keep your head in the same place." I just held onto the saddle horn and didn't say anything.

He took us up little trails, through the woods—I won't say it wasn't pretty, I guess I was just a little uncomfortable with this side of him. And I was uncomfortable because I was being led around on a horse by a Mongol warrior and I was afraid to relax and enjoy it. This seems to be the way it goes for us—some part of me loves it that he just grabs the lead and takes it, carries me away with him... but another part of me is telling me that I'm a weakling, a stupid swooning weakling, for liking it. Does the fact that I turn into Jello when he tops me in bed mean that I'm just supposed to roll over for him in the rest of my life? No, that line of thought isn't fair to him—if I said Stop to anything, he'd stop. It's not that he takes what I don't offer, it's that I'm disgusted with myself for continually offering it, and that it feels so damn good.

Anyway, after a bunch of uphill climbing which my mare had to be coaxed through, we came to a little clearing. He hopped down again—causing me to blush once more from the same memory—and got me off the horse, which was much more of a production. He attached them by long lines to a tree, and then turned to me. "Take off your clothes," he said.

All I could think of was the fact that we were not anywhere with four walls around it to shield the gazes of strangers. "Are you kidding?" I said.

I could see his eyebrows go up, but he just spoke softer, like he was gentling a nervous horse. "There's no one around. I was checking the whole time we came up here. Almost no one comes to this area, except a couple of the riders who aren't there today. We're quite safe. I wouldn't put you at risk, you know." He spread his hands. "If it really scares you, you don't have to. But I thought you might like to fuck out here."

I couldn't tell him that I didn't give a damn about the scenery, I just wanted him so bad I could taste it. But then I figured that the most honest thing to do was just to take off my damn clothes, so I did it. He stripped to his tank top, but kept his pants and boots on. He extracted a handful of leather straps out of the pocket of his *del* and then hung it on a tree. I stood there with my erection free in the naked air, because I felt like it would look even stupider to cover it.

Then he came over and kissed me, grabbing me by the back of my head and shoving his tongue down my throat. "Down," he said, and I went down. "Over," he said, and I went over, ass in the air. Then I felt him pulling my head up by the hair, and starting to put those leather straps over my head. "What the hell?" I asked.

"I thought it would be fun," he said. "If you hate it once it's on, tell me and I'll take it off." His fingers pried open my mouth and settled a leather-wrapped bar between it, and I realized that he was bridling me. I had a sudden flash of panic and I made an incoherent noise, but it wasn't Stop or Don't. I couldn't have talked very well with that thing in my mouth, but I could definitely have made myself understood, so why didn't I? I felt him pause for a moment, and then when I didn't say anything more, he just kept going. I felt the straps wrap around the back of my head, buckle, and tighten with a jerk. Other straps fell onto my shoulders and I realized that they were reins. Then those reins lifted and jerked backwards, moving my head up involuntarily, and my erection got so hard that it was painful. I was so turned on that I forgot to hate my cock for betraying me in that way.

I heard him doing something with plastic that snapped, and then his fingers were inside my ass, opening me up. I've been practicing on my own, so I'm a lot easier to open up these days. It didn't take long at all, which was good because I was worried that just the pressure of his fingers was going to make me shoot off. Then I heard unzipping and felt the head of his cock up against my ass. I am ashamed now to say that I moaned and pressed back into him, that he didn't have to take me at all, that I found his cock with my asshole and slid right onto it. That I almost came right there, but managed with some breathing and contractions to hold out. Well, for all of about two minutes, that is. Two minutes of him yanking back on those reins, the leather bit pulling my head back, and his cock pounding into my ass. I'd forgotten, last week, that he'd shown me his medical paperwork and told me that he was clean. I'd forgotten that he could put his naked cock into me now. Without even touching my cock, I came so hard that I yelled around the bit, but my heavy breathing broke it up into a loud sobbing noise.

He didn't stop, even though I'd come. I wanted to fall back on the ground, my head in the grass, but he was still pulling the reins back and keeping me upright. I squeezed my ass muscles desperately, trying to get him to come quicker. I even humped him vigorously. It never occurred to me to ask him to stop. Then I felt him coming in me, squirting my insides for the first time. It had never occurred to me that I would feel it. You can't tell that sort of thing from watching porn. It made me hard all over again, which would have been useful a moment before but now was going nowhere, since he slowed his thrusts and stopped, his hips still up against my ass. The reins fell slack and my head hit the grass, gratefully.

I could feel him messing around with something, and then he pulled out. I squeaked as the emptiness of my ass was suddenly filled again with something cool and smooth. "What the hell—" I mumbled around the bit, and reached back to feel the smooth flat rubber that was occupying the crack of my ass. I wasn't stupid, I'd seen buttplugs on the Internet and I knew what they were. But I hadn't thought that the first time I'd touch one, most of it would be embedded inside me. I kind of wished that I could take it out and look at it, touch it, see what the rest of it felt like in my hand. But whatever crazed urge keeps me doing all this didn't let me consider the option.

"I thought it might be fun," he said again. "Especially given the ride back." My stomach contracted at the thought, but my goddamn cock got even harder. He unbuckled the bridle and got it off me, and I stood up, gauging the feel of the plug in me. It wasn't really all that uncomfortable—actually, it felt smaller than his cock, which isn't all that huge. Sorry, Erlik—not that you'll ever read this—but you're no John Holmes, not that I mind when you're up my ass or down my throat. Actually, it's kind of nice that I can take all of you without much trouble. "I got the smallest size to start with," he said to me.

"To start with?" I asked, but he just told me to get dressed and he'd help me back up. I could feel the plug as I bent and moved to put my clothes on. Like I said, it wasn't all that uncomfortable, it was just very much *there*. I was aware of it every second. Usually you just forget about your asshole, even if it's sore, and even then you ignore it. With the plug, I couldn't pretend it wasn't there. In fact, I couldn't think about anything else except the fact that my asshole was being stretched—if only a little—by a rubber object that had been shoved up there.

Getting me on the horse was a production again, and the second that I plopped down heavily on the saddle I cried out. Erlik asked, with a concerned face, if I was all right. "If it hurts too much I'll take it out," he reassured me.

At that point I stopped being irritated at myself for being so willing to go along with this, and started being irritated with him for assuming that I was too much of a weakling to go along with it. I don't know how I made that shift—maybe it was implanted with the buttplug—but somehow I realized that rather than evidence of being weak, going through all this with him could be a way to be strong, to show that I could endure anything that he could throw at me. *I can fucking take it*, I almost snarled, but I stopped myself because my mental gyrations were not his fault. "I'm okay," I said, wriggling around on the saddle to get the best position. "It just startled me, that's all."

He swung up onto his horse, took my mare's reins again, and then leaned over to kiss me on the back of the neck. His other hand found my crotch, where my cock was being kept at permanent half-mast by the plug, and said, "You know what turns me on the most? Thinking about the fact that my come is sealed up in your ass by that plug." Then he kneed his horse into a fast trot and I was jerked along, with those words echoing in my head and my cock going from half-mast to full-on all over again.

All right, I need to go take care of something before I type any more here. Just thinking about this is too much.

❈

I am back. Did I shoot come all over the bed? I did not. I stuck the plug back in my ass and got almost to coming, and then stopped because it's still fucking better to come when he's there. And I am not yet ready to say his name while I jerk off. And, stupidly, it seems like a better idea to rebel by not coming unless he's there—at which point I don't have to say his name—than to rebel by saying screw it, I'm not following that rule. God, am I an idiot.

Anyway, the hard part came later. What, that wasn't the hard part? No, that was the fun part. All the way back to the stable, my thoughts alternated between *How am I going to get to the car with no one noticing my erection?* and *Goddamn, there's a rubber plug in my ass and it jolts every time this horse moves, and I've got his come sealed up inside me,* and between those three thoughts of fear and desire was periodic rumination about my newfound idea of turning Erlik's escalating demands into a test of endurance rather than a shameful thing. Yeah, I can see how that could be seen as rationalizing the fact that it's happening and I like it in spite of myself, but it was the first chain of logic I'd found that made me feel better about myself instead of worse. I really wanted to talk to him about it. I still do. Obviously I couldn't, because I could not open my mouth and make it say those things. Not yet. I need to try it out for a while first.

Which was forthcoming, because we went back to his house and the challenges didn't stop. He solved my first worry by getting me off the horse facing away from the gaggle of people between us and the car, and then gave me his *del* to carry. The direction of his eyes told me that he knew exactly what I'd been thinking. The second two problems were not solved until we got back to his tent in the city and I asked, "So when do I get to take this thing out of me?"

"Soon," he said which meant that I would be allowed to take it out, which cheered me. "I have to decide what to do with my come."

That utterly bewildered me. "What?" I stammered.

"Well, I can't very well ask you to eat it once it's been in your ass," he said. "At least not since you didn't get an enema to clean you out first." He smiled at me, as if that was supposed to be reassuring. I was completely frozen by the images that were forming in my mind. *Enema? What the hell? What would that be like? Would he want me to get them regularly? Would he want me to eat his come out of my ass if he'd cleaned me out? How clean was clean? And why the hell is my dick even harder?* Up until now he'd come into a condom and thrown it away. I'd only ingested come that had spurted into my mouth or onto my skin. Apparently the rules were about to change again.

He must have seen the look on my face, because he backpedaled. "That may be a little too advanced a perversion for you," he said. "I'm sorry, it was just a chance comment. Obviously you can go use the chemical toilet." He motioned to the camping toilet in the corner of the tent, next to his jerry-rigged washing system of hanging gallon jugs of water and towels over the concrete drain in the asphalt.

I have come to believe that whenever I get angry, I get stupid. Whether it's at me, at him, or at the world, when that irritation rises in me I just lose my brain and do dumb-ass things. I don't know why. But I'd been turning the idea of our play as endurance training over in my mind for an hour, and now his gentle backing off made me feel as if he was treating me like a weakling. Isn't that what he's been doing all along, treating me like someone who had to be coaxed and gentled and led delicately into doing this? God, I had already told my parents that I was gay, I'd ruined my relationship with my family in order to stake out that territory, and I was too cowardly to just grab it and go with it. Why couldn't I just proudly be a cocksucking faggot who takes it up the ass and just get on with my life?

Of course, I'm not unaware that he's taking me straight from the shore to the deep end, on a pretty fast course. Most ordinary gay men, the ones who don't haunt leather bars, wouldn't be putting a bridle on me and riding me like a mare in the woods, or plugging up their come inside me and making me ride back. But so far he's never struck me or been cruel to me. He's just exerting his control, getting off on what he could get me to do. That's obvious, and even if I've been playing that game with some reservations, I'm still playing the game. And I could probably say no if something was really terrible... but now somehow I've got it into my head that if I'm not a weakling, I shouldn't say no without trying.

The little voice in the back of my head mumbles something about how I've started to think that suffering a little is kind of hot, and reminds me about how, even after I'd come and my erection was limpening and my ass wasn't nearly so interested in being fucked, I kept going. Actually, I humped his goddamn cock like a lust-crazed monkey, remember? Because it was hot. I was being used as a fuckhole and it was damn hot.

I decided in that moment of utter stupidity that if he hit me, I'd say no. That would be my limit. But anything else, I could take. I'd practice my strength on things that didn't actually involve pain. Like licking up his come after it had been inside my ass. For some reason this absurd line of reasoning made sense to me at the time. Maybe the presence of the plug in my ass was drawing too much blood away from my brain, I don't know, but like the moron that I was, I said, "I'll do it."

He looked at me, and I think he wasn't sure what I was talking about. "Do what?" he asked.

I took a deep breath. "I'll eat your come," I said. "Now, if you want."

His eyes widened, and I felt a little thrill that I'd actually been able to surprise him, to be there one step ahead of him instead of being coaxed through every doorway. "You're sure?" he asked.

"I'm sure," I said. "What do you want me to do? Shit it out into my hand? Or into a bowl or something? Or just onto the floor?" The last option, dirty as it was, almost seemed better than the second one, which gave me a flash of dog bowls. Well, I'd already been a horse once today, I reminded myself. That made me grin, and then I really smiled because I saw the look of pleasure on his face. His lips were parted as if I'd just given him the best birthday gift ever. I was playing his game, I realized, with something other than mere reluctance. Maybe not enthusiasm yet, but... active willingness? I think I can cop to that. And that big smile on his face made me want to hug him, to kiss his long hair which was straggling out of its ponytail, to promise him anything to see it again.

I could almost hear his thoughts racing as he turned his eyes away from me. "None of those. Let's strip, and you sit on my lap."

I blinked, but obeyed. He stripped down as well, faster than I did, and sat on the edge of the bed. Then he made me turn around bend over, and he carefully extracted the plug. For a moment it was like a breeze was blowing through my opened ass, and I reached back to touch it. My asshole was gaping open all by itself—not a lot, just enough to slide a couple of fingers in without trouble. Then I squeezed my sphincter, which felt strangely weak, and it started to close up.

Erlik made me sit down on his lap, with his cock slid between my buttocks and pressing up against my balls. Not inside me, just sliding in my crack and slowly becoming harder. "Squeeze my come out of you now," he said. "Squeeze it onto my cock."

And lick it off, was the unspoken command. I was grateful for that. The cocksucking would distract me from any horrid smells and tastes that I would be enduring. I bore down and heard the embarrassing *splort* as I lost his come. Fortunately, I'd taken a shit just before leaving for the stables, and I hadn't eaten much at all that morning, so there was nothing else. He gave my ass a very light slap, signaling me to get up. *Does that count as hitting me?* ran through my mind. *Nah. That was nothing.* I got down on my knees, told myself, *You are not a weakling*, and dived for his nasty, sticky cock.

I hardly noticed any smell or taste, to be honest, partly because he was fucking my face hard enough to make me drool all over myself—honestly, I think most of his come probably ended up going down my torso, but who cares—and partly because I had one hand behind me, fingering my loosened asshole. And of course the fact that my cock was hard again. At the last minute he yanked me off of his cock, turned me around, shoved it in my ass again, and came. Then he replaced the plug once more as I knelt on all fours, gasping and drooling, tears streaming down my face. But I *fucking did it. I fucking did not flinch.*

I felt his hand on my hair, turning me around, giving me tissues to clean myself up. I crawled up onto the bed with him. It was starting to rain outside and the sound pattered on the plastic tarps covering the tent. He was kissing me and telling me how sexy I was, how fucking awesome I was. Then he said it, and at first it jarred me. Good boy, he said. You're such a good boy.

And again I split into two parts, one part swelling with pride— *I was strong, I could take whatever he gave me, and I was a good boy*—and one part thinking, *That is so fucking patronizing and why is it making you feel so damn good?* Before I could get into a really good internal argument, though, I felt his hand on my cock, and the first voice won hands down. "Do you want to come?" he asked me. The second voice managed one *Is that the reward good boys get, you bastard?* before the other voice said aloud, "Yes, yes," and all I could think about was my cock.

He kissed me again, and said, "I'm probably not up to coming again, but I really have the urge to get onto your cock." Another kiss, which I was so dumbstruck that I could hardly return.

"You mean that you want me to fuck you?" I squeaked. I hadn't seriously considered it, because I guess I'd figured that Erlik was top-only. But now that he was saying it in my ear, the proposition began to look really good. I didn't think that my cock could get any harder, but it did. "Um... you might want to stop that, or I'm just going to come," I gasped.

He let go of me. "Not exactly fuck me," he said. "May I tie you up?"

I nodded—what the hell—and he slid over me and got the ropes out from under the bed. My wrists and ankles got lashed to the cot's undercarriage, and he kissed me once more. I wondered if he was showing me some kind of weird solidarity with what had already gone into my mouth, but I didn't care. Then he turned around and straddled my head, and spread his ass cheeks with his hands. "I want to get onto your cock and ride you again," he said, "but differently this time. Do you want this on your cock?" I watched his asshole twitch, so close to my face.

I managed to tell him, through a dry throat, that I did. Actually I think that I would have begged for it if he'd told me to, but he didn't make me go there yet, thank God. "Then kiss it," he said. "I told you that someday you'd kiss me there."

Well, considering what I'd already done, it seemed like no big deal just to plant a kiss on it, so I lifted my head and did that, gently. I heard him sigh in pleasure, just once. Then he got off me and went over to his washing station. I craned my head in surprise, roped down to the bed, but he got a washcloth and cleaned his crack thoroughly with soap and water. Then he came back and straddled my head again. "Kiss me again," he said.

I obeyed. He smelled like soap now, instead of musky sweat. "I've cleaned myself for you," he said. "To about an inch deep at least. I don't think that your tongue can go deeper than that. But if you want this asshole on your cock, you'd better lick it good first."

I admit that I should have seen that coming, but it took me entirely by surprise. *He washed himself for you,* I told myself sternly. *Don't be a weakling. You can fucking do it.* And I did. His asshole was soft and wrinkled and tasted of minty Dr. Bronner's. Then he started moaning, making noises like I'd never heard out of him before, and I liked that. A lot. I wanted to hear him make those noises all night, so I plunged my tongue into his hole and worked it around. The noises continued, and even got louder, so I tried fucking his hole with my tongue, in and out. He pulled away for a moment and moved back, bumping my face with his ballsack. "Lick my balls," he gasped, and I did. His cock had been hanging down but now it was lifting up, getting stiff. He pushed his ballsack entirely into my mouth, which I stretched wide so as not to bite down on it. My cheeks were puffed out like a chipmunk's, but I kept running my tongue along it.

Then it was back to his asshole, and I ate him out for about ten more minutes, during which I think I existed in some kind of pleasant fugue state. My cock was hard, but not so bad that I was afraid of coming too soon. I was restrained and couldn't move anyway, except for my mouth, and my face was pressed into his asscheeks. All my consciousness was in my working tongue, and in listening to him groan. I almost whimpered when he got off me again.

He didn't notice, because he was busy smearing lube on his ass, and then he straddled me again with that quick motion. I felt my hard dick touch his flesh, then press, and then a tight warm wetness slid down over it and it was my turn to groan aloud. He flashed a grin at me. "Feels good, doesn't it?" he gasped as his buttocks hit my pelvis. Actually, it felt so good that I was terrified that I would come again, too soon, and ruin his ride. I made a few hoarse words to that effect, and he just grinned at me. "Think of something that scares you," he said.

I didn't know whether that helped or not. My earlier limit— you won't hit me—leaped into my head. I imagined being tied to a post and whipped. I opened my eyes and saw the wooden ribs of the tent frame overhead, and the image shifted to have me hanging from the beams, screaming as I was beaten unmercifully with a stick. Well, it did help my erection back off a little, didn't it? Long enough for him to bounce up and down on my cock, his hands on my shoulders and all his long hair falling around him, and looking so sexy that he eventually distracted me from my ambivalent fantasy. The sensation of his ass on my cock was amazing, like a tiny hand stroking it while it was buried in soft wet heat. His half-erect cock slapped my belly, and then he suddenly opened his eyes and said, "Come!"

My first thought was, *yeah, sure, like that's just going to happen because you ordered it,* and then I forgot all about that because I was coming. My head was skeptical while my traitor cock obeyed him. As I thrashed around in my bonds, he made a sound and collapsed onto me. I blinked, because I was sure that he hadn't come, but I liked the feeling of his body on mine, my cock softening in his ass and then slowly slipping out. I felt his heavy breathing, but I didn't say anything until he lifted his head and said, "Let me get you out of that."

"Did you... come?" I asked him hesitantly.

He smiled at me, blinking and shaking back his hair, and my heart contracted inside me. "Sometimes I can come just with my ass," he said. "Rarely, and only when I haven't done it in a while. Which I haven't." His eyes went far away and for a moment my afterglow was interrupted for a great hatred for anyone else who had been there before me. But then, I was there and they weren't, were they? He untied me and we lay together, and I mentioned the fact that there was a plug still in my ass.

He nodded against my chest. "You're going to wear it home, where you can do anything you want so long as you tell me about it."

What did I do? I locked the bathroom door, after everyone else had gone to bed. Then I took out the plug, squatted over the tiles, and pushed out his second load of come. Then I put the plug back in and jerked off while I licked it up off the floor, but I didn't come. Why has already been discussed. It's enough to know that I wanted to.

Chapter Seven

It happened the first time that they slept together, curled up in Erlik's new bed. He'd managed to trashpick a double bedframe and mattress that wasn't in terrible shape, and installed it instead of his tiny cot even though it took up a lot more floorspace in his *ger*. They'd told Paj's parents that they were going to see a ball game that would run late, and would be back in the morning. Erlik even stopped by the stadium on the way there. ("I thought—" Paj began, but Erlik cut him off. "We are. But your little brothers and sisters said that they wanted pennants and stuff, so go over to the concession stand and pick some up. Then we'll go back to my place.") They had screwed thoroughly and passed out together under the old sheets that Paj's mother had been throwing out.

Later, Erlik felt grimly that it was no accident that his spirits chose this night to come to him and demand another duty that he had been putting off. He'd been so wrapped up in Paj that he'd pushed away the invitations when they came, subtly, like whispers on the wind before he would fall asleep. He had been shirking, and there would be an object lesson.

The dream was beautiful—he was flying on the wind, a horse thrumming between his thighs. Its hooves did not even touch the clouds, yet he could feel their impact on the blue sky as if it was solid earth. Then the horse slipped away from between his thighs and he found himself flailing in midair. Then he was falling through the sky and clouds, and the earth was rushing up to meet him. For a moment he panicked, twisting around to find where his horse had gone, and then just inches away from the ground he was seized and pulled to the back of another horse. This one was black, and he held onto its mane as it ran across the earth. "Thank you," he whispered into its ear. He knew who it was. It was him, and he never flew, because he was an earth spirit rather than a spirit of the heavens.

"Flying a little high, aren't you?" The resonant voice came from behind him, and he felt the strong body press up against him where the horse's back had been bare of any other rider. He was both the black horse and the man whose face Erlik would see when he turned around. "Tur Khan," he whispered. "I have been flying high. Are you here to tell me that I will fall?"

Two arms encircled him from behind, strong and muscular. He smelled rich earth, sand, some kind of bitter and grassy weed. The sweat of a horse. The sweat of a man. Tur Khan spoke in his ear: "Do you fly so high that you cannot come down to earth for me?"

Erlik ducked his head in shame. "I will always come at your call, my lord," he whispered.

"Perhaps I might like you to come when I do not call," he said. "Perhaps I might like it if you would seek me out." There were a hundred shades of nuance behind his tone—desire and threat, amusement and grimness. Erlik shivered, feeling the electric-fence sensation in his spine that came with the presence of the spirits, multiplied ten times over as Tur Khan halted the black stallion and helped him down. The horse was gone as soon as Erlik's feet touched the earth, and there was just the spirit-man with the great mane of black hair shaved high on the sides, his bare chest glowing in the diffuse sunlight, clothed in vines that grew up around his body. With one hand he tore away the vines as if they were a curtain hiding his magnificent naked body, and with the other he tore away whatever was clothing Erlik, who hadn't even been aware that he was wearing clothing until suddenly he wasn't.

Tur Khan did not attack him, but then he never had to. Erlik was on his knees in a moment, opening himself to the spirit-man whose feet seemed to grow into the earth. A great hand seized him, and another seized his erect cock, stroking it into a fever pitch. He cried out as he was penetrated by a shaft that burned like fire and sang like the reverberation of a bell inside him. "My lord!" he called out at the moment of orgasm, which shook him awake. The great arms around him receded and he felt himself lying flat on his back in his new bed, breathing heavily. His cock buzzed with the aftershock of coming and there was wetness on his belly.

When he opened his eyes to the pale dawn light beginning to seep in through the netting window, he saw Paj huddled up against the fabric wall of the tent, as far away from him as he could possibly get.

A variety of things to say ran through his head, most of them designed to lead Paj away from the truth, and he dismissed them all. This moment had to come sooner or later, and he knew what trouble lay on the other side of disavowing his spirits, even if only a little. "Good morning, Paji," he croaked out.

Paj just stared at him.

Erlik struggled to a sitting position, wiping the stickiness off of his belly. "What did you see?" he asked, trying to keep his voice neutral.

The young Hmong man's lips moved soundlessly for a moment, and then he licked them and said, "I woke up because you were making noise and moving around. I figured it was a wet dream, and I figured I would join in... you know, wake you up with a blowjob or something." He stopped and swallowed. "But when I tried to reach for you, I... couldn't. It was like my hand wouldn't go there."

"And that was all?"

Paj shook his head. "You'd kicked off the covers. I could see your... see your cock, all hard. You were moving your hips." He gestured vaguely to the air. "But it was more than that. Your cock was... was moving in a weird way."

"How weird?" Erlik whispered.

"Like...." He took a deep breath. "Like someone was touching it. Like your foreskin was being pulled up and down." He looked away. "Then you spread your legs. I could tell when you were dreaming...." He paused again, and then decided to continue the thought. "Dreaming about being fucked. You were shaking, in a rhythm. Then you came." It was almost an accusation. "And I couldn't get near you. Every time I tried, it was like my body would freeze up, even though my mind was screaming. I tried to convince myself that it was a dream. But it wasn't."

"No," said Erlik quietly. "It wasn't a dream.

"It wasn't a dream for you either, was it?" Paj asked.

"No," said Erlik. "It wasn't."

"What the hell was that thing?" Paj looked shaken, and angry. "A ghost?"

Erlik sighed and reached for the bottle of water next to the bed. "Hardly. A ghost would have been easy for me to fend off. That was a very powerful spirit—you might think of him as a minor god, even. Tur Khan, the male principle of the fertile earth, the black horse."

"Why was he...." Paj trailed off.

"Fucking me? Because he comes and does that sometimes. Off and on. It's hardly an unknown thing among the shamanic traditions of the world," he added. "Some people even marry their spirit-lovers. I don't think any of them want that from me, though. Even in a gay way."

Paj just shook his head and looked away. "I don't know if I can deal with this," he said, withdrawing further into himself. "I mean, being lovers with you is one thing. Even bringing home some other guy, I could deal with that. But invisible people... I don't even know if I believe it."

"If you don't believe it, then there's no problem, is there?" Erlik snapped. Paj wouldn't meet his eyes, and he sat up with a quick flash of panic. "Listen, Paji. Nothing has changed. I told you at the beginning what I was. Hell, I told you while you were lying there with a bullet in your leg. This is what I do. You knew that already." Silence. "Please talk to me. Please." He tried not to sound desperate.

Paj twitched. "But I didn't think it was real," he said.

"If you had believed it was real, would you have refused to suck my cock?"

He could see the young Hmong man relent a little. "No. I still would have sucked your cock. I probably still would have let you fuck me. But—"

"But what?"

Tears suddenly welled up in Paj's eyes and his words came out in a rush. "I can't say no to you," he rasped out. "I want to say no—I mean, not all the time, just sometimes you go a little fast, and I want you to slow down but I can't. I can't tell you to stop. And if your spirits are real..." he trailed off, and then set his jaw, "...then maybe they're doing it to me. Maybe they're making it so I have to go along with whatever you want."

The breath whooshed out of Erlik in one long sigh. He wanted to jump to reassure Paj of that, to say anything that might comfort him, but his eyes shifted involuntarily to the altar on the other side of the room, and his mind replayed how he'd acquired Paj in the first place. "That's a fair question," he forced himself to say, and Paj's eyes flew to his face in bewilderment. "I don't know the answer, and I wish you'd told me about this earlier, if it was bothering you."

"There was no point in telling you if it was just me being neurotic," Paj sniffed, and Erlik handed him the box of tissues and then took a deep breath.

"I can check on it," he said. "If it's true, then I'd want to know anyway. It would mean that...." *That my conquest of you wasn't really a conquest. That they had thrown the game for me, and stolen my victory before I'd even begun.* "...That you wouldn't have been giving me your full consent on everything, and I don't want that. I want you to choose to be with me, not to be forced." He held his hand out across the abyss between them, and to his relief Paj reached out and took it. He pulled the other man to him and held him, tight. "Believe that. Believe that I never want to force you."

"How are you going to find out?" Paj asked into his shoulder.

"Shagai." As the other man raised his head, he smiled. "You've never actually seen me read, have you? Not a problem. If there's one thing I *can* do, it's to find out if there's been spirit meddling." Shoving himself reluctantly out of the warm bed, he spread a couple of sheepskins on the floor and grabbed his bag of knucklebones off of the altar. "Come on down here. If it's too chilly for you, you can bring a blanket."

"It's not cold, it's June," Paj said, slipping out of the bed and awkwardly sitting on the other end of the stretch of skins. "What do I have to do?"

"Nothing. You sit there. And I ask." Erlik snagged the stone bowl and the juniper incense from his altar and lit it. "I have to smoke the tent, sorry. *Hurai, hurai, hurai*. Golden-edged Golomto, daughter of heaven, I ask your blessing. *Hurai, hurai, hurai*." He traced the juniper stick in the air, breathing in its clean evergreen scent. "Now I ask this of you, Gods and spirits: What bonds have you put on this man in front of me? What do you move here with your hands?"

He could see Paj's expression, trying desperately to look skeptical, as the bones rattled in his hand; but as soon as they fell Paj leaned over to look at them. "What do they say?" he asked in spite of himself, then looked embarrassed.

"One horse, three sheep. That means that you must do it yourself." He swept them up, rattled again, and dropped them. "Four goats. Delay, slowness—it will all happen very slowly." One more catch and throw. "Four sheep—luck will come, but after a long time." His hand stayed over the thrown bones for some time, listening for the message, hearing only laughter. Finally he relaxed, and his mouth twitched upwards.

"What?" asked Paj again, anxiously.

"They aren't making you do anything," Erlik said. "It's all your choice."

Conflicting emotions sped across the young Hmong man's face, finally to be replaced with sheepishness. "Oh," he said. "So it is all just me being neurotic."

"It was a fair thing to worry about, given the situation," Erlik said mildly. Inside, he felt foolish himself. *Worrying so hard about whether this was a real conquest! What the hell.* "I know that the spirits did actually pull some strings to bring us together, but now it's just up to us to make it work... or not."

"I kind of wanted it to be them forcing me," Paj said, glancing quickly up at Erlik from beneath his falling bangs.

"But it's not," said Erlik in the same mild tone. "So where does that leave you?"

Paj sighed. "Wanting you. For real. And, I guess, wanting to be your...." He trailed off.

"My lover," said Erlik. "This is a bad thing?" He mimicked the Yiddish accent of a Jewish professor they both knew, and Paj had to laugh in spite of himself. Then his face sobered.

"Your bottom," he said. "Your... sub?"

"Submissive," Erlik said. "Yes, that's the word."

"But not your slave."

A small shrug. "I haven't asked for that. I've only asked for what you're willing to give me." He scooped up the *shagai* and put them back in their leather bag.

Paj seemed to consider that for a moment, and then crawled forward across the sheepskin to put his head on Erlik's knee. "Okay," he said. "Let's talk about what I'm willing to give you. I think I can do that now."

Chapter Eight

Online journal, June 29:

Well, after he did the reading for me, I felt a lot better. Apparently it was just me being neurotic. So I started to fix that immediately by actually opening my mouth and talking about it. We didn't have much time left that morning, but the next time we met, we started with a discussion of my fears.

"I don't want any of that pain stuff," I told him. I felt somehow satisfied, rebellious even, at being able to enforce that boundary. "I mean, I can't even imagine what it would be like to... to like that."

He just looked at me for a moment. When he does that, I can almost see the wheels buzzing in his head as to how he's going to make me go along with something. This time, however, he called my bluff in a bigger way. "So you don't understand how someone could like it," he said.

"Yes."

"And you're afraid of it."

"Who wouldn't be?" I shot back, then I felt like that was rude to all those people he knew who weren't, apparently, afraid of it. "I mean... isn't it normal to be afraid of pain?" That was probably also some kind of insult, but I couldn't figure out how to say it any other way.

He nodded thoughtfully, and then got up out of the bed. "All right," he said. "I'd like to show you something. It doesn't require any pain on your part, but you'll need to do what I say. Get up, please." There was a clipped formality to his voice that unnerved me, but I got up. He took the belt out of his discarded pants, folded it in half, and held it out to me. "Take this, please." I did.

Then he climbed back onto the bed and knelt, facing away from me, his naked ass in the air. "Hit me," he said.

My jaw almost fell onto the floor. "Wha-at?" I could hardly speak, and I absolutely couldn't move. "Why?"

He looked around his shoulder at me. "Because I want to show you, from the other side, something about how this works. It would be better if we had a real masochist here to show you, but we've only got me, so me it is. Don't worry, I've done this before. It's not something I crave, but... anyway, I want to show you what it's like. Please. Just go ahead and hit my ass."

Well, it wasn't like he was telling me to do something that would hurt, was it? I swung half-heartedly and the belt made a light slap against his butt. "Harder than that, please," he said, and I felt irritated. That made my next swing significantly more sprightly, and he gasped and turned his face into the bed for a moment. I froze, watching him, not sure what I'd done. Then he lifted his reddened face and said, "Again." And I gulped and did it.

I don't know how many strokes of the belt he took by the time he finally stopped me—thirty, maybe? How many times did he choke out, "Again!" and grip the bedclothes, his whole body jerking with each blow? By the end of it, I was ready to beg him to stop, but not because I felt that it was terribly wrong. It was because my traitor cock had gone hard on me, and bounced every time I swung that belt. I had to hold it with my other hand to keep it from bouncing uncomfortably, and the urge to rub it was overwhelming. Finally he gasped out "Enough!" and I dropped the belt instantly.

He panted for a moment, rocking back and forth on the bed, and then lifted his face again. "Tell me what you've done to my ass," he said. "Tell me what it looks like."

"It's all red," I said, "with red welts on it. Like striping."

"Touch it," he said. I reached out and cupped his buttock, ran my hands over it. "Tell me how it feels," he said.

"Hot," I said, not meeting his gaze. I kept my eyes on his ass instead, hot and red and... what? Sexy? Well, yes, of course it was sexy. "I can feel the heat, and the stripes are like ridges."

"Squeeze it," he said, and I did. He gasped, whether in pleasure or pain or both I couldn't tell. His cock was coming up to half-mast, though. "What do you want to do to it?" he said, in a low, intense voice.

I flushed hot and my hand froze on his reddened ass. "To lick it," I whispered, "...and to fuck it." I'd never said that before, but right now I desperately wanted his swollen, welted ass. It simply begged to be fucked. It begged to have a cock shoved into its puckered hole and have the body attached to that cock slammed into it again and again, the hands attached to that body grabbing that abused flesh. *You are a pervert,* I told myself. *You are a fucking pervert.*

Well, yes. Why didn't I figure that out earlier?

"You want it?" he grated out harshly. "You want it? Say it."

I licked my lips and tried to make my voice steady. "I want to fuck your ass," I said.

"Then do it," he said, then added in a lower voice with a grin that was half grimace, "But make sure you lube me up, all right?"

I dived for the lube and squeezed some of it out with shaking hands, my breath coming rough and fast. For the first time, I gently slid my fingers into his ass. It was surprisingly relaxed. *Well, he's had gods fucking him, after all.* I got in two fingers, then three, then lined my cock up to his ass and pushed in the head. It was only the second time that I had ever had my cock in there, and it was completely different from the first time, and yet he was still in control. I was just following orders, and it freed me. I was free to grab handfuls of his hot assflesh and yank him back and forth on my cock, even though he cried out. After all, he was the one in charge. If he had a problem with it, he'd tell me to stop, and he didn't. He just moaned and whispered obscenities, egging me on. I pounded into his ass until I was as close as it was possible to get to orgasm and still be able to hold back. "Can I come?" I gasped out.

"Yes," he hissed. "Come in my fucking ass. Now." I felt my balls contract and I shot into him, hearing myself groan into the still air in the tent. He slid forward until he was lying face down on the bed, and I slid down on top of him, kissing his shoulders and upper back.

"Thank you," I whispered in his ear.

He turned his head toward me, eyes still closed. "Was that good for you?" he asked.

"Yes," I said. "It was great. It was really great. But I know that I only got it because you allowed me to have it."

"Do you see why I would want it?" he asked.

That was the moment the lesson zinged home. I hid my face in his hair and didn't answer for a moment. "Do you like it?" I asked. "I mean, it didn't make you hard while I was doing it."

"I'm not a masochist," he said, "but it does have certain effects afterward. Sometimes... it's worth doing, even though it doesn't make me aroused during the actual act. It's good for other reasons." He paused. "Among other things, it reminds me that I'm strong."

Another arrow followed the first one into my heart. I clutched him, still hiding my face. "I want to give you that," I said, and with a sinking feeling I realized that I meant it. "But I'm still scared. Really scared. That I'll hate it so much I won't be able to hold through. That I'll fail you because I can't make myself like it."

He shimmied out from under me and turned over, taking me in his arms. "Those are fair concerns," he said. "The answer is to go very, very slowly, and to turn back each time while you can still freely give it. I can't really push that boundary for you. I mean, I could try, but I don't think that would be good for you. I think you should push it yourself."

I looked him in the eye for the first time since he'd gotten up off the bed and offered me his ass to beat. "How do we start?" I asked.

An evil grin suddenly lit his eye. "Well," he said, "you can start by taking care of your cum. Remember the rule?"

I blushed and moved away from him, and he got up and squatted over my face, ready to sit on it with his beautiful hot red

Chapter Nine

ass cheeks so that I could eat my own come out of it. "Yeah," I said. "That's a good place for a pervert to start."

True to his word, Erlik started slowly. It began with the occasional slap on the butt while his cock was hard, or while he was getting fucked. He even warned the Hmong youth—"I'm going to smack you now." And then the smack, and then it was over and they kept on with the sex. Then once while Paj was on his knees sucking his cock, he gave a warning and lightly slapped his lover's face. Paj sputtered and came up off his cock. "Was that a real problem for you?" Erlik inquired, in as dry a tone as possible given the state of his erection.

"Yes—no—I mean, I almost bit you! What if I had?"

"Well, that would be the price I paid, wouldn't it? Don't worry, that had occurred to me."

"What if I drew blood?" Paj seemed indignant, then softened. "I don't want to hurt you accidentally," he said in a quieter tone.

"We're sharing body fluids now," Erlik said with a wicked grin. "I could always shove my cock down your throat and hold it there until you choked on my blood." The sudden widening of the other man's eyes gave away his arousal at the idea, and then he blushed. "Let's try it with more warning," Erlik said. "Put your mouth back on my cock, but let your jaw hang loose. Soft mouth." Warily, Paj took Erlik's cock back into his mouth, and Erlik gently took hold of his head with one hand and slapped his cheek with the other. "Let yourself drool, it's OK, the floor's asphalt." He switched sides, slapped a little harder, then a little harder still. When Paj winced, he stopped immediately. "Now go back to sucking."

After he'd come, Paj crawled back up onto the bed and snuggled in next to him. "That wasn't so bad," he said. "And I could tell it turned you on."

"I would guess so," Erlik said, "considering that you had your mouth on the barometer."

"I liked how you held my head when you did it," Paj continued, a little shyly. "That made me feel... like you didn't really want to hurt me. Or—um—I mean—"

"Like I cared about you?" Erlik said. "And the juxtaposition of being cared for and being struck... how was that for you?"

"Weird," Paj said. "And kind of nice. Like when you tie me up—I'm helpless, but it's all right to be helpless." He paused, evaded Erlik's eyes, then took a deep breath and said, "Hold my head now. And do it again."

Erlik's hand snaked around the back of his neck, and he kissed Paj's forehead, and then almost tenderly gave his face a light slap. Paj's breath drew in, but he didn't say anything, so Erlik slapped him again harder. Then a third time for good measure, and then he stopped and kissed him again. *Better to leave them wanting more than to think they've had too much.*

"I... could take a little more than that, I think," Paj whispered as their lips parted.

"And next time you will," Erlik promised, pushing Paj's head back down to his chest. *Next time you'll wait for it, half with fear and half with anticipation. Next time you'll feel proud to have taken more. And the time after that, you'll be vaguely disappointed if I don't do it, pretty boy, because you'll remember that confluence of pride and desire and excitement and you'll want it all over again.*

The next day, Erlik was accosted in the college parking lot as he was parking his bike. "Yo, Eric!" a voice called out from behind him, and a car door closed. He froze, and then forced his fingers to uncurl from the handlebar of the bike. Turning around, he stood with his head high, not responding. Just watching. He was glad that he was wearing his new *del*, that his hair was tied on top of his head in traditional style, that at least he looked clean and neat and not homeless. The young man in the polo shirt who had just gotten out of the Honda Civic stared at him with a contemptuous curl to his lip. Beyond him, Erlik could see the middle-aged woman driving the car, with the sunglasses and headscarf over her permanent.

"So what is this, a new kind of drag?" his brother Kenneth sneered. "You think you're impressing anyone, wandering around in a Halloween costume pretending to be Genghis Khan?"

"Ask him about the newspaper photo!" the woman shrilled

from behind the car windows. That was the way his mother often worked—send one of her children to confront unpleasant things while she yelled perfectly audible orders from the car or the next room. Erlik supposed she must mean the photo from the newspaper article, months ago. He'd figured that word of it might have filtered all the way back to the town where his family lived, but he'd rather hoped that the difference in name and his unusual appearance would have prevented them from ever making a connection. No such luck. He gave his brother a blank, expressionless look. For all the talk about Asian inscrutability, he seemed to be the only one in his family who'd ever been able to pull that off. "Good morning. May I help you?" he said blandly, as if they were total strangers. He gave them a slight, perfunctory bow.

Ken's hostile expression deepened. "You can tell us what you're doing, running around claiming crazy things. Saying you're a fucking Mongolian!" Silence from Erlik, who clasped his hands together behind his back so that Ken wouldn't see his fists clench, and continued the blank stare. "You know, you can get away with this stupid stuff while you're in college, but eventually you're going to have to live in the real world, you know."

"Bringing shame on the family!" his mother screeched from the car.

Erlik unsealed his lips, finally. "My name has been legally changed," he said. "I am no longer part of your family." *Especially when you threatened to kill me, or get me raped by the football team as a lesson, when you found out I was gay. Especially when Mom and Dad stood there taking your side. I left that night and never came back, and you ceased to matter to me.* He took a deep breath. "Actually, about eight percent of the men in central and northern Asia are descended from Genghis Khan. I am. So are you. I had my DNA tested." Ken's face had turned from hostile to bewildered. Erlik took another breath. "The old man got around. Now, if you'll excuse me, I have classes to attend." He turned on his heel and walked away toward the building in front of him, which didn't contain his classroom, but would get him out of the parking lot.

"Faggot!" he heard Ken scream behind him, "Fucking faggot, you're going to die of AIDS, you asshole!" His mother's high voice echoed something, but he couldn't make it out. It didn't matter—he'd talked about being queer in the newspaper, after all; it wasn't as if anyone on this campus didn't know about him. Eric Chang had died, he told himself, months ago. He was Erlik Solongo the *buu*, and that was all that counted. *The past was over*, he told himself. *The future remains to be plundered.*

The incident brought up another nagging thought in his head, though, and he spent the periods between classwork turning it over and looking at it. It was Uncle Gavia who'd given him the idea—*go to him, boy, he might help you. If you are respectful enough. If you take his advice, because old men like that. If you can convince him that you are not a fraud. He can lead you through the mire to find your way to the other side.* But it was still a stomach-churning proposition for him. It was one thing to know that one was truly a shaman when one was faced with unbelieving or credulous Americans. It would be quite another to face down someone who had their own relationship with the spirits, and had given himself to them for decades before Erlik had even been born.

Go to him, whispered Uncle Gavia, but Erlik wasn't quite ready yet. *Give me a couple of weeks*, he whispered back. *Or give me the courage to do it.*

The courage is in your lover's eyes, Uncle whispered back, or perhaps it was the golden breath of Golomto. It rippled up his spine, and that night when he went to see Paj, he picked up one of the Hmong-English newspapers that were discarded by the door. They weren't for Paj's parents, but for his younger sisters to keep their hands in both languages. He found the ad in the back, and the next morning called for an appointment. Luckily, the man spoke a little bit of English. Otherwise it would have been charades or an interpreter, and there was good reason to keep all the Hmong-speaking people with whom he was personally acquainted well clear of this mission.

Before Erlik approached the apartment building and knocked, he bowed and said a prayer of blessing to all the spirits who might be within, or watching. He had the odd sensation of feeling his own spirits, normally shadowing him on such a mission, hang respectfully back as he knocked on the door. It was opened by an erect, dignified old man in traditional clothing, supporting himself with a gnarled cane. "Phia Xiong?" Erlik asked quietly, and the man nodded.

In careful Hmong—Paj had taught him, at his request, to say it for his parents—Erlik said, "May your house be blessed with peace and prosperity, and your family flourish." The old man's eyebrows went up—Erlik might be Asian but he was clearly not Hmong—and he switched to English. "Sir, I am a beginning shaman of the Mongolian ways—a *buu*—and my spirits say that I should come to you. I need the advice of your spirits about a family of your people. Will you ask them for me?"

The old man regarded him rather expressionlessly, but Erlik knew that stare—he was looking with eyes that were not in his face. He took in the box dangling from Erlik's hand, which was cut with airholes and occasionally emitted a muffled clucking noise. It was traditional to bring a chicken for sacrificing when visiting the *txiv neeb*, or spirit-master—the Hmong name for their shamans. Finally, he nodded again. "Come in, come in," he said in heavily accented English, making shooing motions with his hand. Erlik entered and passed under the dangling protective beads, and the door closed behind him.

"We're going on a road trip to where?" Paj had said, incredulously. "We could be going to Tahoe, for heavens' sake. Why some stupid little state in the middle of the country?"

"It'll be fun," Erlik said. "And we're going because I have

business there. And regardless of where in this country we drive, there will be motel rooms. Right?"

"And you can afford this how?" Paj asked skeptically.

"A client wants me to drive to him, and he's paying for our travel expenses," Erlik told him. "I need a lot of professional equipment that I'm not willing to trust to airline baggage handlers, so he's renting the car for us. You can drive, right?"

"Well, yeah, I can drive," Paj said. "Although I've never done marathon eight-hour drives before. But why do we have to drop everything and go now?"

"Because he may not live out the month," Erlik said simply, and Paj shut up. Actually, there was another motive for Erlik's hurry to see his client; there was an event happening in that Midwestern state that he desperately wanted to surprise Paj with. Then, of course, there were all those motel rooms, and maybe a leather bar in another state. He'd avoided bringing Paj to the local bars; some part of him perversely wanted to keep them as his own hunting grounds, just in case.

He picked up the rental that next morning, and then picked up Paj at his parents' house, duffel in hand. They put on music and drove throughout the day, and found a cheap motel as the purple evening was beginning to fade out to black on the horizon. Paj walked in and looked around. "You know," he said, "I've never actually been in a motel room before. I've never slept anywhere but my home and your tent. My family doesn't travel much."

"Then let's create some good memories," Erlik grinned. "Get your clothes off and get on your knees." He began to tug off his tank top; the July air outside was sweltering and both of them were in shorts and sleeveless shirts. Erlik had even packed his boots and was wearing a cheap pair of sandals. Not terribly sexy, but it was a day for bare feet. Paj seemed to think so as well, because for once when he dropped to the floor, he spontaneously kissed Erlik's toes. Then, as Erlik's pants came down, his mouth came up and fastened itself like a leech all the way to the root of Erlik's still-soft cock.

With an indrawn breath, he fell back onto the bed, happy to

let Paj's mouth take care of him. Wrapping one lithe leg around Paj's neck, he forced him deeper onto the stiffening cock that was beginning to choke him. There was something wonderful about feeling one's cock literally grow down someone's throat, Erlik thought briefly. Paj had become an amazing and versatile cocksucker—perhaps that first time in the hospital bed had imprinted on him somehow. Erlik put his heel on the back of Paj's neck and pressed the young Hmong man's face into his groin. "Take that cock," he gasped. "Fucking swallow it." He felt Paj's throat muscles close convulsively on the head of his cock, and then he moved his foot and let his lover gasp and breathe. He idly wondered how many breaths he ought to let him have, but after two deep gasps Paj threw himself back onto Erlik's cock again.

After about twenty minutes of brutally fucking Paj's face until he could feel the man's drool running down his thighs, Erlik pushed him off. "Put your head on the floor, between my feet," he ordered. "Breathe. Get yourself ready, because I'm going to mess with your cock next."

Paj visibly swallowed, his reddened eyes on Erlik's, and then slowly lowered his head to the floor. His ribcage expanded with a few deep breaths. Erlik put one bare foot on the back of his head, and he didn't object. They waited there together for a couple of minutes, and then Erlik stepped over him carefully and unzipped a duffel, pulling out several hanks of rope and cord. "Get up and lie down on the bed," he told the motionless Paj. "On your back. Don't move."

Within another couple of minutes, he had the young man's hands tied behind his back, and his ankles spread and secured to the cheap motel-bed headboard. Then he unwound the cord and began to tie it around Paj's cock and balls. He'd done a little genital bondage before with Paj, but this time he didn't stop until Paj's balls were two bright pink spheres protruding from the coil of cord, and his cock was tightly bound halfway up its length. Paj stared at his magenta cock in only slightly horrified fascination. "See what I've done to you?" Erlik told him. "Don't worry, I'll take it off before it does any damage. But it feels so much more sensitive, doesn't it?" He ran his hand up the bare, swollen section of Paj's cock and his tied-off balls, and the other man threw his head back, moaning.

"Fuck," he gasped. "That feels... fuck."

"That's exactly what I'm going to do to you in a little while," Erlik said, "but first I have other plans. You know, some guys experiment with this sort of thing when they're young kids, exploring what they can do to their junk." Erlik's mouth twisted in irony and Paj wondered feverishly exactly what he meant. "Oh well. See how this feels, now." He bent forward and slid his mouth down the bound cock, and Paj's groaning grew even louder, accompanied with a string of surprised obscenities. It was the first time that Erlik had put his mouth on his lover's cock. Instead of going fast, he teased it leisurely with his tongue and lips, making Paj thrash around in ecstasy. He received a light slap for that—"Hold still or you don't get any more!"—and his cock and balls were taunted with light oral strokes until he didn't know if he would spontaneously come, or just be kept at a frustrating high forever.

Before he could come, however, Erlik suddenly brought him out of his floating state with a light slap on the side of his cock. His eyes flew open and he made a surprised noise. Erlik smacked his cock again, a little harder, and he jerked. "Wha—" The young shaman gave him an evil one-sided grin.

"You can say no," he said. "In fact, if that was horrible and about to break you, now's the time to speak up."

Paj gritted his teeth, recognizing the challenge for what it was, and torn between anger and desire. His rock-hard swollen cock was making it difficult for him to think straight about anything. "Damn it!" he grunted, struggling against his bonds. Several emotions flashed across his face.

Erlik watched him like a hawk, poised to act. When nothing more than a few incoherent noises came out of Paj's mouth, he smacked his cock again. This freed the young man's voice to yell, but no words came. "Well?" Erlik asked again. "Do I keep going, or do I stop?"

His partner breathed heavily, closed his eyes for a second, and then opened them again to stare into Erlik's eyes. "Give me something to bite down on," he whispered, "and don't hit my balls. My cock, okay, but not my balls. I don't think I could...." He trailed off.

"Right." Erlik nodded once, picked up his discarded underwear, and stuffed it into Paj's mouth. Then he touched the side of his face, gently; his hand ran down Paj's underwear-stuffed cheek, and he said, "I'm right here with you all the way. Just spit that out and tell me if it's too much." They locked eyes, and then Paj nodded and closed his. It was as great an act of trust as Erlik had ever been given, and he was suddenly moved to kiss the other man on the neck, and then to move his mouth once more to that tightly bound cock. Paj hadn't expected that sensation, and he squirmed, making a surprised noise and thrusting upward. Erlik held his pelvis down and mouthed his cock some more, and then came up off it and smacked it again.

He went back and forth like that, sucking it gently and then slapping it, watching Paj moan and squeak around his gag by turns. The young man thrashed and sobbed, but didn't stop him. After each round of sucking, the slapping got a little rougher, but as soon as Erlik saw him really struggling it went back to cocksucking. Then, when Erlik had judged him to have had enough, he quickly untied Paj's ankles, positioned himself between the young man's spread legs, and lubed his ass. It took no more than a few seconds for his fingers to slide in with no resistance, and his hard cock followed immediately upon their withdrawal. It was the fastest he'd ever gotten into Paj's ass, and he hadn't given him more than a few thrusts before that bound, purpling cock spurted and its owner screamed around his gag loud enough that Erlik was worried for the people in the next room.

Paj's chest was heaving and tears were leaking from his eyes, so Erlik decided not to keep fucking him after his arousal was gone. He quickly undid the string around Paj's cock and gave it relief, and then he went to pull out, but Paj spat out his underwear and gasped, "No, don't! Keep going. I want to feel you come in me. I want to feel you come."

Erlik smiled, his half-soft cock suddenly hard again, and hefted Paj's asscheeks in his hands. Then he gave Paj what he hoped would be the fucking of his life, pounding into him until he had to stuff the underwear back into his mouth, out of fear of bringing the management over.

❖

The next morning Erlik went to his client's house, dropping Paj off at a downtown station with orders to meet him back in four hours. The young Hmong man didn't like to show it, but he was honestly excited at the idea of being able to explore a strange city with no strings attached, if only to wander around and observe. When Erlik picked him up in the early evening, he was grinning and talking nonstop about his day, and all the things he'd seen. Erlik was uncharacteristically quiet and let Paj run on; his client was terminally ill and wanted to check with the spirits on what loose ends he should tie up in his last days, and where he should leave his estate. Sometimes the job was the opposite of a fun time.

When they got back to the hotel, Erlik told Paj to dress for a casual party. "We're going out at around six-thirty. We'll pick up some food on the way, in case there's nothing but chips and dip over there."

Paj's eyebrows went up. "Who the hell else do you know in this town?" he asked.

Erlik's eyebrow flipped up and down with his shoulder in a kind of shrug. "You'll see."

"Hmmf." Paj mock-scowled at him. "Mister Mystery Man. OK, fine. But the food better not be too awful."

The shaman gave a wry, preoccupied smile and pointed at a tangle of woods behind the hotel. "I'll be there for a while," he said. "I need to talk to a few People." The way that he pronounced the last word gave it a proper-noun connotation. He scooped one of his shaman-bags out of the back seat and loped off. When he returned, Paj was waiting for him in their motel room.

An hour later, they pulled up to a municipal building awash in cars. "Good-sized party," Paj commented.

"I hope so," Erlik commented cheerfully. "I'd hate to have brought you all this way for nothing." He grinned at his partner and got out of the car.

Paj followed, more reluctantly. "This is one of those kinky parties, isn't it?" he asked, trying to sound gruff but betrayed by the waver in his voice. Still, he followed Erlik up to the propped-open safety doors, and then stopped in surprise. Several people pushed past him, their black almond eyes fixed on the crowd inside, chattering in something other than English. Paj stared at the sign next to the door and swallowed. *Shades Of Yellow*, it read. *Hmong GLBT Association*. He turned to Erlik, unable to speak.

"Well, come on," his partner said, obviously enjoying himself. "You're not going to let me go in there alone without a translator, are you?" He turned and headed in, aiming himself for the snack table.

Paj swallowed again, shook his head, and followed. As usual.

Chapter Ten

Online journal, July 26:

A week left before we're back in school full-time again. My brain was all over the next semester, my last until I graduate. Actually, I probably wouldn't graduate if it weren't for him, especially after getting shot. It's been a while since I've written anything here, because I've been trying to let things settle in my mind and figure out where I am with this crazy situation. After all, it's not like I can take my issues with our relationship to a therapist. What would I say? "Oh, he's a shaman, and I was all paranoid that his spirits were forcing me to do whatever he says, but he took some knucklebones and checked with them, and it's not them, it's just my own mind that's convincing me that I ought to follow him around like a puppy and spread my ass for him. And I told him that I didn't want him to hurt me during sex, but then I rescinded that boundary because I just want so bad to give it to him, and because it proves that I'm strong. Oh, yeah, and because I beat his ass and it was really hot. I find myself wishing that I was a woman, because then I could just be his submissive housewife and no one in my family would care. But of course then I wouldn't be with him anyway because he's gay. And I feel guilty because men aren't supposed to want that, even the gay ones. So what do you think—am I crazy?"

The Shades of Yellow gathering was a real turning point for me. I got to talk to a lot of people in the same boat with regard to their families, even if they were halfway across the country. The consensus was that half the respected elders in any given community were cautiously for the existence of GLBT people, and the other half were not. Half of the younger people there were still trying to convince their families that it was all right, and the other half had been thrown out or disowned or had given up and walked away. It brought up the conundrum that I'd been avoiding—would I give up my family for my lover? I asked myself that, for real, for the first time that night while I lay awake in the motel bed and listened to him breathe.

The answer was easy and clear. *Yes, I would.* I backed up, startled, and ran myself through a series of vignettes—never seeing my parents or my little brothers and sisters again, being outcast in the world, living with Erlik in his tent in some asphalted back yard— but it kept occurring to me that my siblings would grow up and might seek me out on their own, and never seeing the rest of my family again just didn't seem to be as frightening as it had been. I was on financial aid for my college anyway, so that was assured. Of course, before Erlik came along, I'd been seeing it as being thrown out on the street with no one... and those final vignettes about living in Erlik's tent with him kept resolving into pornography, so I finally gave up and started beating off. Then I got the idea to sneak under the blankets and start sucking his cock as a way to enhance my masturbatory experience, and he woke up and there wasn't any more thinking for a while, just bodies.

The next day, though, I'd made up my mind. I would wait until I was confronted again on the matter—no point in making trouble—and then I would tell them that I loved Erlik and was going to be with him, and if they didn't like having a gay son, I'd pack my things and be out that night. To hell with the family honor. To hell with the family, even; although that thought made me unaccountably sad. But when I tried to talk to Erlik about it on the drive home, he was just silent, and then told me not to do anything rash, that he had something brewing and it was going to come to fruition soon. Something to do with my family. Something that he couldn't tell me just yet.

"Why not?" I asked, almost in tears. "Don't you trust me?"

He got all grim-faced and said, "Spirits." Then he wouldn't talk about it any further.

That set me back a notch. I hate it when he deals the shaman card. Especially now that I believe it. I remember that feeling of reaching out toward his writhing body and being *stopped*, just like someone had grabbed my wrist, except that I couldn't feel a hand on me. Whatever he's done, I am terrified to get in the way of it. I'm still not ready to pray, though—I may believe in his spirits, but I guess I don't believe that anything would listen to me.

We drove in silence for the next hour or so, listening to the radio, and then suddenly Erlik drove off the road into some state park. When I asked what was going on, he said something about the mountain spirit having signaled him, and he needed to stop and talk to it. He rummaged in the back seat for some juice and crackers for an offering and then vanished into the woods. Half an hour later, her returned, and apologized in a preoccupied manner. "It's going to be like this," he said wryly. "It's the way my life goes."

"Yeah, I know," I said. "My aunt married an ER psych doctor. He brings his work home with him all the time too." I grinned at him, if a bit crookedly, and he grinned back and suddenly leaned over and kissed me, and everything was all right again. Then Erlik pulled the car over into a more secluded spot and pulled me into his lap, and we had a brief, violent bout of sex that left me gasping. I couldn't get my pants down fast enough to climb onto his cock, so he grabbed my head while I was struggling and forced it down into his lap. I choked on his cock, feeling my own get hard as I frantically yanked my shorts down to my knees. I could feel the breeze coming through the partially open window onto my bare ass, but I didn't even think about how exposed I was. All that mattered was his cock. And then his balls, as he pulled his cock out of my mouth and pried it wider, and pushed his ballsack in. "Lick me," he growled, and I lavished tongue on it, my cheeks bulging out like a chipmunk's, not caring about the lack of dignity. Then I was pulled up and positioned across his lap, facing away from him.

I had worried about where we were going to get lube, but it turned out that I didn't need any—there was, for once, enough drool and spittle on his cock, and enough lube left inside me from last night to work. He held me from behind, working my cock with his hand, as he banged up into my guts. His other hand reached around me and cupped my balls, ringing the top of my ballsack with his fingers, simulating the way he tied up my balls. They bulged in his palm, helpless in the air, and the feel of it made me come all over the steering wheel. Seconds later, I was on my knees again, with him shooting into my mouth. He grabbed me by the hair, opened the door, and dragged me across his lap. "Spit it out," he ordered, pointing at the dirt, and I did it, glad that I hadn't swallowed him yet.

"It's for the mountain spirit," he said afterwards, as I stared, blinking and gasping, at the bushes outside the window. "He likes sexual energy, probably from all those young campers. I figured that it would be an easy enough offering."

"Such a perv," I said. "Happy to help any time."

Chapter Eleven

Somewhere between dreams about failing the new semester in school, Tur Khan came for him again. Erlik was wandering through the halls looking for a classroom, and then a door opened onto wilderness. He stumbled through and then saw the black horse running in the distance. His belly tightened with a visceral longing, and he began to run, knowing even as he did so that there would be no way to catch him. However, Tur Khan enjoyed a certain amount of pursuit. It proved how much you desired him.

At some point he decided that he'd had enough and stopped running, calling out, "My Lord! If you would have my company, please stop for this mere mortal!" Before he could finish the sentence, the horse was trotting up to him, and then it was shifting into the great muscled man that he knew, the face that Tur Khan showed him. The spirit-man laughed and opened his arms, and Erlik went into them. Tur Khan embraced him and then stepped back, taking Erlik's chin in his hand. "Will you open to me?" he asked.

"Always," Erlik told him. "It is an honor." And then Tur Khan's hands were all over him, and he was thrown to his back into the long waving grass, under the wide sky. The sun was blotted out momentarily by the demigod's bulk, and then his great cock was thrust in front of Erlik's face. He opened his mouth and felt it slide in, stretching his jaw painfully but not more than he could handle. He choked on it, but found a way to breathe anyhow. Spirits were good at that—giving just enough struggle to make the experience real, while making sure that it would not flow over into a loss of one's arousal. After all, they *wanted* your sexual energy—there was little point without it.

Tur Khan knelt over his face, fucking it as he'd fucked Paj's mouth earlier that week. It was an artful, graceful dance, the great cock sliding down his throat and then retreating to stroke his lips. The rhythm speeded up as Tur Khan began to bellow, trumpeting like a horse in rut, crushing Erlik's face beneath black-furred pubes. Then the pulsing, fizzing divine essence was coursing down his throat, running through his body like liquor or drugs, making him convulse with ecstasy as it always did. It couldn't really be considered a physical orgasm so much as an energetic explosion, ripping through his meridians like touching a high-voltage wire.

He barely had time to breathe before Tur Khan was flipping him over, turning him onto all fours. "Be my mare, boy," the deep voice rumbled, and Erlik pressed his face into the grass in a position of reverence. One of the reasons he preferred to be the dominant party in his human relationships, besides it being his general personality, was that having sex with divine spirits was more than enough bottoming for his life. He'd gone ass-up for Paj to show him the ropes, but he'd been in control all the time. With the Gods, control was beside the point.

"Open yourself to me," Tur Khan commanded, and he reached back and spread his asscheeks wide, revealing his hole, which pulsed and begged for Tur Khan's cock. There was no need for him to speak; he knew that Tur Khan could read the message imparted by his ass, better than words. He felt the head of that great cock at the opening of his ass and sighed with pleasure, then cried out with the intensity of the sensation as it slid in. It wasn't pain so much as just a huge stretching, feeling like he would be cored like an apple, like it would slide out his open, drooling mouth. Tur Khan's cock never behaved like a mortal cock; it was impossible to gauge how big it was at any given time.

Impaled, he moaned and let go of his ass, needing both hands to brace himself as the earth-spirit pounded into him. One hand grabbed his hair, keeping him from sliding away. The fucking felt as if it were easily displacing his internal organs, filling him entirely, making him into nothing more than a sheath for that cock. He wondered briefly if Paj, or anyone that he had ever dominated and fucked, had ever felt even remotely similar on his cock. Certainly no human being had ever made him feel like that, but then he didn't respond in this way to human beings. Tur Khan had been the first one to sexually dominate him in his teens, and no mortal dominant had impressed him since.

He felt the impossible weight of the earth-spirit's body pressing him down into the grass, and he gave up trying to hold himself up. Flattened between earth-energy and earth-energy, he floated on the writhing impalement in an altered state of ecstasy, coming awake only when he felt the fizzing, sparkling energy of Tur Khan's seed filling him from the other end. This time, his orgasm was much more physical, and he knew that his sleeping body had spent its seed as well. The great cock withdrew from his body, leaving him feeling hollowed out and emptied. He expected Tur Khan to go then—he would lift his head and see the great black horse running off into the sunrise—but to his vague surprise, the huge black-haired man stayed, sitting beside him on the grass.

"We must speak," he rumbled, and Erlik turned, startled.

"My lord?" He dragged himself to a sitting position, the world still spinning.

"The little pup your Uncle has found for you," Tur Khan stated.

Erlik was suddenly alert. "Yes, my lord? What of Paj?"

"He has made a bargain with the pup's ancestors. That is why all went so well with the spirit-master's reading."

"Yes, I'm aware of that."

"But what you do not know is that you must pay for it," Tur Khan told him. "The deal is struck, and even if the pup runs away, you must pay for it."

Erlik shivered, and nodded. "What must I pay?"

"You are lucky," Tur Khan said. "You live in a time when those such as you may walk in the sunlight, may live honestly. In older times, survival was more important. You know this. You know how they had to hide, to lie with wife to get children, even when it was not their way."

The young *buu* bowed his head. "I know this, my lord."

"The pup does not come by this through no means. He inherited it through his father's side. His far-back ancestors—*those* ancestors— they want a taste of what you have. You must give it to them."

Erlik swallowed. "Yes, Tur Khan. I will give it to them. When? How?"

"Awake, and you will know." Tur Khan touched him, briefly, and then he found himself rising as if through deep water, gasping for breath as he opened his eyes and stared at the cracks of light coming from the flaps in his *ger*. It was past morning, and he had a whole day free, ahead of him. Paj had a dentist appointment, and he had expected to spend the day running errands. Sighing, he pulled himself out of bed. Apparently there were more important things to do.

There are many tools for those who work with spirits to use, Erlik's Uncle taught him, again and again. None are called to every tool, but if something works for you, use it! Use it for offering, use it for sacrifice, use it for payment, use it to take yourself into the place between the worlds. And if what lies between your legs is something that works for you, use it! The rules set up by others as to what you can do with it, they do not apply to you. If you are one who is called to that gift, do not waste it! Your sex is tool, is doorway... is offering. Do not hesitate to use it.

It was that teaching which had led him to Tur Khan. It was that teaching which led him to this moment, kneeling naked on the sheepskins in front of his altar. "Hurai, hurai, hurai," he muttered as he smoked the room with juniper. "Uncle, send them over. I am ready. I will give what must be given." Then he sat quietly and opened his inner eye, and waited.

It did not take long. There were three of them, coming forward hesitantly, cautiously, not trusting that this time it was all right. The first one came toward him on feet that did not touch the asphalt. With one touch, he revealed to Erlik a lifetime of memories—shy, quiet, he had done what he was told, always. He had married and sired children, and then taken hard to drinking. He had died from falling drunkenly into a ditch, despairing and miserable, unable to speak of his desires to anyone.

Erlik caught the long-dead man in his arms. He did not know his name, but it didn't matter. This one needed gentle loving, and while that was not necessarily Erlik's thing, he could manage this once. The dead man collided with his energy body, giving strange almost-sensations to his physical flesh. Erlik kissed him, touched him, found his cock between his thighs, gratified by the gasp made with that gesture. He took the dead man's hand and led it to his own cock, showed him how to touch it. He had already made himself hard before beginning—there was no point in offering a gift to the spirits without displaying it well.

A ghostly hand ran itself over his cock and balls, in that searching, exploring way of a man who has longed to touch another man in this way, but has never had the chance. He shivered, thrust himself against the faint tentative touch, felt it solidify against his energy body. He was so used to tuning into his energy body until its sensations rang in his mind nearly as strong as those of his physical flesh—a legacy of all that sex with divine spirits—that he could follow that thread of faint touch without trouble. "Harder," he whispered. "Rub harder, if you can." He concentrated on clenching his own hand around the dead man's cock. An invisible breath ruffled his hair, and he breathed with the dead man, synching his living breath to the rhythm of the Dead. He willed the man to feel his desire, his joy in the initiation. *Let it pass between us like a hot wire. I am sorry, friend, that I was not there in life to give this to you. I would have done so, with all my heart.*

It didn't take long—the long centuries of waiting saw to that— and the ghostly figure writhed in his arms, arched and spasmed, and then turned soft and sated. He reached further for Erlik's cock, but Erlik shook his head—it was too soon to come just yet. He would need that hard-on for the next two. Three ancestral spirits, he had been told, would come to him nine times each. If he would lay with each one nine times, they would make sure that Paj's family would yield. He smiled as the first dead man dissipated into the darkness of the ger. Most gay men, in this situation, would simply encourage their lover to abandon his family and run away. For him, though, it wasn't that simple. Uncle had been unable to do anything about Erlik's family. If something could be done to spare Paj that pain, he would do it.

The next dead soul came out of the darkness, kneeling before Erlik and begging, wordlessly. This one knew what he wanted— he had seen some soldiers raping another man, and while he knew that it had not been pleasurable for the weeping victim, he could not stop thinking about it... or masturbating to those thoughts. Night after night he had fantasized about the soldiers coming for him, discovering that he was a man who wanted men, and abusing him accordingly. *Use me*, he said silently. *Take me. Make me struggle and yield to you.*

Erlik got to his feet, snapped his fingers, and pointed to his still-hard cock. The man moved hesitantly toward it, and he seized his noncorporeal head and thrust it onto the hard shaft. Since he was already dead, he couldn't suffocate, and Erlik forced his cock down the ghostly throat over and over. He could just barely feel the man's head, with its long hair; he focused on burying his hands in it and trapping the dead man's face in his crotch. *After all, it's not like he can suffocate.* When he tired of that, he pushed this second ghost down on all fours and took him by the hips from behind. Taking a deep breath, he focused himself and his arousal, and deliberately searched for the sensation of the dead man's buttocks pressing into him. Then he moved his hips until he felt the right place, the point of opening, and drove into him.

A cry that only he heard echoed through the ger, and for a moment he paused out of habit, wanting to make sure that the dead soul was not suffering too much at his hands. However, a wave of frustration roiled up as he paused, and so he plunged in again. This man wanted a proper rape, then; no quarter given. He growled deep in his throat and slammed himself into the ghostly ass, fucked it as brutally as he was able. Like many bottoms he'd been with, the man cried and moaned while being entirely absorbed in his own experience. In a way, Erlik was just a prop to his long-denied fantasy. It was satisfying anyway.

On a whim, Erlik pulled out, although the dead man turned his head and cried out in frustration. Erlik laughed at him, deliberately coarse, and pulled his head around to use his mouth again, just as brutally as he had used the dead man's ass. After a few minutes of that, he went back to his ass again. Then back and forth between the two ends, one after the other, until finally he came in the dead man's ass. He hadn't intended to come, but it had all gotten the better of him. Physically, his come sprayed across the asphalt floor. Energetically, it showered the crouching dead man with his life force. As he did it, he had the feeling that the ghost had climaxed as well. The ethereal body convulsed on his cock, and then slid away.

The ghost raised himself up, nodded, reached out a hand and briefly touched Erlik's feet, then was gone. Erlik sighed and looked down at his cock. Maybe he could get the third ancestor to take a rain check to another day? After all, he had promised them all nine times apiece.

No, came Uncle's voice. *You must give to all three at least once, to seal the bargain. You must show that you are willing to give of yourself. What you are asking seals off a descendant's line. It is not to be taken lightly.*

"Yes, Uncle," Erlik breathed, bowing his head, and then looked up. The third ghost stood before him, a wavery shape between himself and the altar. As he squinted, the figure became more clear—and the stab of rage and desire made his guts clench. This man was angry, even cruel. He had been thwarted in his longings, and in his resentment he had hurt people. The image of a young boy, raped, crying, came to Erlik's mind, and he almost retched. *Give me willingly what he would not.* It echoed through the tent like a cry from far away, even though the ghost stood close enough to reach out and touch. *Give me willingly what he would not.*

Erlik set his teeth, breathed, willed himself to remember Paj. *Remember how you feel about Paj, how much you want him to be with you. Don't think about servicing this man eight more times afterwards, just focus on the one time. They didn't promise you that the clients would be nice, just that it would be a fair deal. After all, you are asking a lot.* He bowed his head, his long hair falling forward. *I will yield to you,* he silently told the ghost, whose impatience was palpable.

The next moment, he overbalanced and fell backwards, onto his back on the sheepskins. The dead man had pushed him down. There was much more force, much more presence, in this one. His rage had kept him stronger and more focused on the material world. Like a cloud of hot, wrathful pressure, the dead man was on him; he could smell the musk of a naked male body in the throes of arousal... and smoldering ashes, and hate. His hate was directed as much at himself as at everyone else. Erlik could taste the hot bitterness of his hate as ghostly fingers pried open his mouth and thrust an ethereal cock into it. He surged up as the cock choked him, but his wrists were pinned down by the dead man's hands.

For a moment he considered fighting back—he was a shaman, he could easily pull some of the ghost's life force out and leave him weak, pry him off and throw him back through the door of Death... but a bargain had been struck. *Give him willingly what the others would not,* he told himself, and forced himself to relax and be passive. He could still breathe, although his physical throat kept closing spasmodically when his energetic throat was stuffed full by the man's violent thrusts. *You're not entirely unfamiliar with shapeshifting,* he reminded himself. *You can do something about this.*

Taking a deep breath, he focused on his throat chakra. *Open,* he told it. *Open wide, wider than my flesh, and let him in. You are a hole to be used.* The pressure abated; the thrusting of that ghostly cock was just as hard, but his mouth was loose and took it easily. Knowing what was probably coming next, he reached under himself to prepare his ass. *Do what must be done.* This would be an entirely different experience from opening himself to Tur Khan. He must guard against absorbing the man's rage and tightening up. His hand moved to his cock, which was beginning to respond to the face-fucking in spite of everything.

Then the cock was out of his mouth, and he quickly turned over before he could be spread and taken like a woman. Better to be facing away, better not to look at the man's anger and hate like a miasma between them. He felt ghostly hands touching his ass, but nothing else. To his surprise, he felt a pang of wistfulness come floating through the air between them.

"Yes," he said, thrusting his ass higher. "Go ahead and take me. I'm ready for you. I'm willing. It's all right. For once, it's all right."

A sound between a grunt and a cry forced itself from his throat as the dead man rammed himself in. Being fucked on the energetic level didn't have the same physical force as bodily penetration—for one thing, it didn't require lubrication—but he could definitely feel it. The ghost cock's cold violence filled him, and took the breath out of his lungs. He pressed his face to the floor, panting, and made himself open up. *Focus. Relax. Your energy body can open to this. You can be like the ocean, yielding and unhurt, surrounding everything. You can take everything in him and not be harmed by it. You know you can. You can do this.* He wasn't sure, for the moment, whether the inner voice was his own or that of some other spirit, guiding him through it.

Ghostly hands gripped his shoulders, stroked down his back. His guts cramped with the presence of the dead man's cock, and he forced himself to breathe through it. One hand found his cock, and he began to stroke it again to hardness—the coldness of the ghostly cock had shocked it a bit, but like a trooper it recovered. This wasn't really the sort of thing that turned him on—while he'd bottomed occasionally, it was only to certain sorts of people, and not to ones for whom he had no respect... like this cruel, raging dead man. Still, the weirdness of the situation appealed to him in some way. If nothing else, it was truly perverse, and at the end of the day, Erlik was still a pervert. He laughed, softly, in spite of himself.

This enraged the ghost, and Erlik felt blows raining down on him. They didn't hurt all that much—he was too psychically armored for that—but he realized with a keen stab of insight that this man wanted, needed, the pain in the one he was fucking. Closing his eyes, Erlik nodded. *I am a sadist as well. I understand. How could I not?* He allowed himself to cry out, to feel the pain a little more, or at least the discomfort. The feeling of the cock inside him became more intense, and then he heard the moan with his inner voice.

And then he was empty, and the dead man was weeping. He slumped to the floor and rolled over, looking up at the place where the ghost had stood. He was a roil of confusion, shame, the ashes of all that rage. There was less of it, though. It was as if some of that hatred had drained itself away into Erlik's ass. He felt flushed with warmth all over; better than he had in a long time. *Well, part of being a shaman is transformation,* he thought to himself. *There's no energy in the world that can't be transformed, after all.*

The dead man faded away, and he allowed himself to think for a moment about the future. *I wonder if eight more times will be enough,* he thought. *Enough to drain the hate out of him, to give him some peace in the end. Well, there's more than one way to elevate the ancestors. They say that it took a hundred years of shamans praying to pull the rage out of Chinggis and make him a demigod. I wonder if any of them ever tried this?*

Chapter Twelve

Erlik had been cool enough when he'd called on the phone, but Paj had been with him for months now, and he was beginning to develop a prickle at the back of his neck when Erlik was planning something. He'd called to say that he was coming over with some little gifts for Paj's parents—he often brought them small gifts of food or flowers—but he'd asked casually before he'd hung up whether they had any plans to go out tonight. Paj's internal alarms all went off, although he couldn't put his finger on exactly what had tripped it. Still, he sat on the couch with wave after wave of fear going through him, watching his little sisters do their homework. They were, all three, some of the most fearless kids he'd ever met, always jumping into things without a second glance. He'd inherited all the fear in the family. His mother said that he'd inherited the soul of a relative who had died in the refugee camps, or been killed by the regime they had been fleeing.

His thirteen-year-old sister Shua glanced up at him. "What's wrong, Paj?" she asked in English. "Long face, huh?"

"Nothing," he grunted. He knew that she knew about him—she was old enough to have heard his fights with his parents last year, and understood them—but she just shrugged and went back to her work. "Erlik not coming over?" she asked her math book.

"He's coming," Paj said. "...Soon."

"He's awfully cute," she said, and his two other sisters giggled. "In a weird way. Once you get past the strange clothing." They giggled some more.

"It's not strange, it's—"

"Mongolian, I know." She cut him off. "It's okay. I like him."

It was spoken as if to give him a sort of seal of approval. Just then the doorbell rang, and Paj leaped up and ran for it, before Shua said something unwise.

Erlik's small, secretive smile greeted him as he opened the door... and there was someone else, behind him. Paj stepped back, startled, to see Phia Xiong, the *txiv neeb* that his mother had consulted so often. It had been a few years since Phia Xiong had been in their house at the same time as Paj, but he recognized the wrinkled old man's face. The two of them swept past him, Erlik in his best *del* with his hair slicked up and all his shaman jewelry, the old man in his own traditional outfit. For a moment Paj could have sworn that the air crackled around them, then he shook his head in confusion and forgot the thought.

Erlik's eyes lit on Shua. "There you are. Just who I was looking for." He dug out a twenty-dollar bill and held it out to her. "I need you to do some translating for me, and I'm prepared to make it worth your while if you are willing to be one hundred percent accurate."

The money vanished. "I'll be accurate," she said, showing all her teeth.

"Hey," Paj began, faintly. "I can translate—"

"Not this time," Erlik cut him off, and then his parents were coming out of the living room, and there were greetings all round to Phia Xiong. Erlik asked Shua to ask her parents if they would be willing to speak to him and the old spirit-master, and there was some more polite chatter before they went off to the other room, his younger sister caught up in Erlik's tow like a tractor beam.

It can't be what I've been afraid of, not with Phia Xiong brought along, Paj thought with some relief. *It must be some sort of spirit thing. Maybe an ancestor needs appeasing. My parents will like that, at least. But why my sister....* He wandered in after the small crowd, trying to tell himself that there was nothing to worry about.

Erlik began appropriately, bowing first to Paj's father and then to his mother, wishing each of them blessings and prosperity to their households. Shua translated, her eyebrows cocked with curiosity. His parents nodded—one of the ways Erlik had been able to win them over was through his willingness to treat them with old-fashioned formality and courtesy, even if he was a dirty Mongolian with the face of the hated Chinese. Then Erlik took a deep breath, squared his shoulders, and said, "I wish to speak to you today about your second-to-eldest son Paj, whose life I saved from the murderous maniac." He did not look around at Paj, who felt his stomach lurch downwards. Shua's eyebrows went up even further.

"As we all know, Paj is a boy who prefers boys." Erlik's words fell into sudden silence, on suddenly frozen countenances. He continued, "I am sure that this fact has concerned you greatly, because you are worried for him, and you may fear for his future."

Paj's lips twisted bitterly. *Actually, they're more worried about the family's reputation, and that they won't get any grandchildren out of me, than for my future,* he thought, but Erlik was leaping ahead. "Because I also worry for Paj, and because I believe that the spirits sent me to save him for good reason, I went to consult Phia Xiong. I have asked him to consult his spirits and the spirits of your family line, as I have consulted mine. We are here to tell you what has been decreed."

Decreed. The word fell on them, from his sister's lips—or the Hmong equivalent—and eyes widened. Erlik turned and bowed slightly to Phia Xiong, and the old man began to speak quietly in his rough, low voice. His back was to Paj, but the Hmong youth could make out most of the words. The spirit-master informed Paj's parents gently that the boy was to be given as a wife to the man who had saved his life. The spirits had decreed it, and the omens had confirmed it.

Paj choked, literally, the noise flicking the eyes of both his parents briefly to his face. He wondered what they were seeing. He wasn't sure, himself, what he thought of this. One part of him was howling at the indignity of these two men in their variously embroidered outfits, their ropes of beads, deciding his life as if it was all settled. Wasn't that the whole point of being modern and independent? You were supposed to choose your own future. He'd dreaded the idea of the eventual parental showdown, but he realized that some part of him had secretly been anticipating it.

The other part of him, though, wanted nothing more than to scream "Yes!" Images flashed through his head of going with Erlik to Mongolia, living with him on the theoretical horse farm—which was currently nonexistent, but having seen Erlik in action, he had no doubt that it would eventually manifest. After all, hadn't he manifested this moment? *I want to be with him. Of course I do.*

The conversation had suddenly degenerated into a rapid back-and-forth between his parents and Phia Xiong; Shua had tried to translate, but had quickly given up, shrugging at Erlik. Paj thought about saying something, but realized he didn't really have anything to say. Anyway, Phia Xiong was winning. He was used to arguing down traditional couples. Yes, it was irregular, it was against the usual order of things, but the spirits had decided it. Finally they subsided, and for the first time in the conversation both of Paj's parents turned to stare at him.

In the moment of quiet, Erlik spoke up again. "I promise that I will take good care of your son," he said, nudging Shua to begin translating once more. "He will never starve, or lack for anything."

Paj's lips twitched. *How are you going to promise that, Mr. Buu? Especially when you live in a tent in someone's back yard?* But his father, obviously casting about for something more to express his disgruntlement, asked about the dowry and the bride-price, and who was going to pay for the wedding. That was old-fashioned even for him, although Paj could see how he didn't want to get stuck paying for the gay wedding. Erlik assured him that there needed to be no dowry, and though tradition might dictate that the bride's parents would pay for their share of the wedding, since the bride was not a traditional one, he would pay for it himself. Phia Xiong leaned forward to admonish Erlik that the wedding had to be done right by Hmong standards, and Paj's mouth twisted. *You don't know what kind of expense you're getting yourself into, honey.* His next thought was, *So I'm a bride, huh? How's that going to work?*

❖

By the end of the evening, however, his parents had come around to a level that was astonishing to him. Part of it was Phia Xiong, part of it was that Erlik had brought gifts of traditional food for his prospective in-laws... and perhaps part of it was just that they were glad to have a way to dispose of their black sheep, a way that could be foisted onto the txiv neeb to explain. Either way, the entire thing was settled before Paj got around to saying anything, and then they were eating dinner together, with Erlik sitting across from him.

Paj felt strangely shy with him suddenly, and realized that the Hmong-raised part of him understood that appropriate behavior for one's betrothed was very different for one's friend. They wouldn't be able to have nearly as much unsupervised time between now and whenever the wedding was held, he realized. Not if they wanted to keep the delicate balance of conditional approval with his parents... and he it occurred to him that, stupid or not, he did want it. Erlik seemed to understand that as well, because he left with little more than a careful bow to his fiancée. An image flashed through Paj's mind—being fucked up the ass by this man who was acting the formal stranger—and he smiled ironically at his lover.

The next day they met at the university cafeteria, and Erlik pulled him behind a Coke machine and grabbed his ass. "So, are we getting hitched, or what?" he asked.

"Do I get a say?" Paj folded his arms, but didn't move from Erlik's grasp. "It sounded like you and Phia Xiong and my parents worked it all out between you. It didn't seem like my opinion mattered at all. By the way, how the hell did you get that old man to tell my parents that the spirits said we were supposed to be together?"

Erlik dropped his hand, and for one moment Paj saw the absolute steel in his eyes, the look he got when he told Paj to do something and it literally threw everything else out of his head. The look he got when he talked about the spirits. "Because it's true," he said. "I went to Phia Xiong so that my spirits could talk to his spirits, and make sure. Frankly, the offerings I'm going to have to make to your ancestors will take me a lot longer to pay off than the costs of the wedding. You're going to be an expensive bride."

A chill went up Paj's spine. "So the spirits say that I have to go along with this?" That was an entirely different ball game from merely having one's life organized by busybody humans. He remembered Erlik in the arms of his spirit-lover, and his stomach clenched.

"Not at all. You still have a choice. I made sure to leave you consent." Then his implacable expression gave way to one of hurt. "Don't you want to marry me?" he asked. "I mean, if you hate it, we can always get a divorce. You'll be on your own by then, and—" He was cut off by Paj's lips on his.

"Of course I want to marry you," he whispered as he pulled back. "I want to suck your cock until we're old and gray. It's just that, well...."

Erlik's eyes were shining, but his mouth twisted with humor. "You would have liked to have been asked first? I thought about it, but I was afraid it wouldn't work, and I wanted to give you some plausible deniability, if it was all my idea."

Paj rolled his eyes and chuckled. Later, as they sat in a less crowded corner of the cafeteria, he suddenly remembered something. "You know, you've never actually told me that you love me," he said. *It shouldn't matter*, he thought. *It's just a stupid thing. But somehow it does.*

Erlik nearly choked on his sandwich. "You're right, I haven't," he said. "I... suppose we're both guys, and we were both raised Asian, so it just didn't seem like something that was... I don't know... appropriate to say?"

His partner laughed. "I see what you mean. It's not like I've said it either." There was silence for a moment between them, and then Erlik leaned forward and said in a low, intimate voice, "Do you need me to say it? My gift for whom I begged the spirits. My mare. My little cocksucker. My treasure. My fuckhole. My boy. My buttslut. Do you need me to say it?"

Paj was silent for another long minute, and then whispered, "No."

Then he put his hand gently on Erlik's crotch, under the table, and lowered his eyes. He knew that the shaman would.

About the Author

Raven Kaldera is a Northern-Tradition Pagan shaman, herbalist, astrologer, transgendered intersexual activist, homesteader, and founding member of the First Kingdom Church of Asphodel. He is also a teacher of BDSM spirituality, and an educator and presenter on many topics. He has written (or co-authored) many dozens of books, including nonfiction on paganism, sacred traditions, and alternative relationships, and fiction, including the erotic fiction collection Extraordinary Deviations, also published by Circlet Press. 'Tis an ill wind that blows no minds.

Other titles you may enjoy from Circlet Press!

Faewolf by D.M. Atkins & Chris Taylor
$6.99   ISBN: 978-1-88586-567-0

Faewolves, like werewolves, can walk among men. What happens when Kiya White Cloud, a young gay college student in Santa Cruz, wants one of these men enough to risk his heart–and his life? A paranormal m/m erotic romance from Circlet Press, Inc.

Like A Prince: *Gay Fairy Tales*
edited by Cecilia Tan & Rachel Kincaid
$5.99   ISBN: 978-1-885865-84-7
Five gay fairy tales that feature classic stories with a queer twist. What are the erotic possibilities of the dashing princes and dark forbidden forests that we learned about as children? Includes stories by Elizabeth Schechter, Julie Cox, Kiernan Kelly, Alexandra Erin, and Monique Poirier.

Sea Turtle Inn by H.B. Kurtzwilde
$6.99   ISBN: 978-1-61390-099-4
The Sea Turtle Inn is a hotel/bar once frequented by pirates. Now, paranormalist Drew Wells has been hired to investigate its haunting. Yet even as he learns more about the inn & its history, Drew finds himself more intrigued by the enigmatic proprietor Davis, whose secrets may prove key to finally putting the spirits to rest.